What people are saying about Linda Lochard

"The book draws you into the story immediately, sharing the struggle of a young woman's adventure into the hardships of traveling west. One feels her strength and commitment to the adventure she has begun. I can't wait to see how her story unfolds."

Maie Grynick Nadig

"I got pulled into the story right away, and could easily imagine being there. I am eager to read the full story."

Dr. Larry Nadig

"On May 14th, 1844, my family left Tennessee for the 'Land of Milk & Honey – the Oregon Territory.' We dug our roots deep into Oregon. I am a HUGE fan of anything Oregon Trail and a big romance novel reader. Linda Lochard has lived the trail. Her writing brings to life the toll on the women who made the journey and the hope that kept them going. I hope you enjoy the journey."

Mary Neal-Ireland-Hambleton
5th Generation Oregonian
Author & CEO of Soul Canyon Training & Development

"Linda has been one of the biggest champions of the Applegate Trail's history. From the first time I met her while we were both in the tourism industry, she was always sharing historical tidbits and stories, including her own trips following the path of the trail. I even had the opportunity to participate in a pioneer wagon in a parade in Rogue River that Linda organized. I had never been on a wagon before, so it made a significant piece of Oregon history come alive for me. Because of Linda, I know a lot more about the Applegate Trail due to her bona fide enthusiasm for this history."

Dawn Rasmussen
Chief Résumé Designer
Pathfinder Writing and Career Services

"Linda Lochard has been there and done that! In 1997, she won the Governor's Heritage Tourism Award, recognizing the part she played in bringing recognition to the Applegate Trail through road signs and markings, as well as wagon train re-enactments celebrating both the Oregon Trail sesquicentennial in 1993 and the Applegate Trail sesquicentennial in 1996. I was fortunate to serve as a member of the Applegate Trail board along with Linda, who, as quartermaster, was responsible for many of the major details of the 51-day trek—making sure there were water and food for the animals, campsites and signage, permissions to be on public and private lands and, her special touch, asking each County's sheriff's posse along the way to escort the wagons through their County. During those years, she was truly living in the 1800s. Her expertise and attention to the life details of the early wagon train settlers are profoundly evident in the pages of *Life Along the Applegate Trail*."

Lyn Hennion
Member, Applegate Trail Coalition

"Riveting, raw... exposing the price to be paid in the relentless pursuit of what could be."

John Howell

"Captures the unrelenting daily challenges of reaching for the dream of a new life."

Dale Everson

"Combine heart-warming romance, treacherous terrain, anxiety of the unknown, and hope for a better future, and you've got the key ingredients in this historic western adventure that's beautifully written by Linda Lochard. She masterfully weaves the harsh realities along The Applegate Trail as a wagon train made its way in 1847 across plains, mountains, and rivers where bears and cougars lurked, all with the vision of settling on the pristine land of Oregon. She composed this novel after re-enacting the trip in a real wagon train to celebrate the event's 150th anniversary. Linda's engaging, suspenseful storytelling puts names, faces, and interesting personalities on this rugged peek back at history that's entertaining and educational all at once. If you love to witness the power of the human spirit to find love and hope while following dreams despite fear and danger, then you need to read *Life Along The Applegate Trail: A Tale of Grit and Determination* by Linda Lochard. You will be delighted!"

Elizabeth Ann Atkins
Two Sisters Writing & Publishing

LIFE ALONG THE APPLEGATE TRAIL

A Tale of Grit and Determination

Linda Lochard

For information about this title or to order other books
and/or electronic media, contact the publisher:

Atkins & Greenspan Publishing
TwoSistersWriting.com
18530 Mack Avenue, Suite 166
Grosse Pointe Farms, MI 48236

ISBN
978-1-945875-93-9 (Hardcover)
978-1-945875-94-6 (Paperback)
978-1-945875-95-3 (eBook)

Printed in the United States of America

Cover and Interior design: Van-garde Imagery, Inc.

All photographs and maps used with permission.
All uncredited photographs and maps courtesy of the Lochard Family Collection.

"Courage is one step ahead of fear."

The Honorable Coleman A. Young

Dedication

To my Mother, Wanda Bigham, who always encouraged me and had faith that I would complete this book.

To those early pioneers who traveled west without any knowledge or guarantees as they went forth, with only a dream, grit, and determination.

To the many who participated in the reenactments of the trail 150 years later and provided me with fodder for this story.

Acknowledgments

It's so hard to believe that it will be 25 years ago that writing this book became more than a thought, and eventually, Chapter One. Never did I think about all that it would take to complete it. I've said many times, to as many people, "Writing my thoughts was the easy part; now the real work begins."

My thanks go to many, and I'm sure to miss someone. I'll start with the basics in thanking my parents, Wanda and Harvey, for teaching my brothers and me that we could do anything we put our mind to. The trick being, "Don't quit until you're finished, and to realize when that is." My Mother was happy to oblige reading the first third of my manuscript, even before it was edited. Rough stuff. Unfortunately, she did not get to see the publishing of my book, but without her, I may not have continued.

Thanks to my older brother Steve—an avid hunter with first-hand knowledge about bears and other wildlife—I didn't have to go out and wrestle a bear or chase down a wild turkey to write about them.

To my close friends and past co-workers, thank you for supporting my efforts and always having a hand on my shoulder, urging me on. Several have shared their thoughts in the form of testimonials, never intimating the possibility that I would not meet my goal of delivering my novel.

Thanks to local authors Anne Schroeder, Jane Kirkpatrick, Doranne Long, and longtime friend and author, Dawn Rasmussen, for their willingness to offer direction in this process. They were willing to share some of their earlier challenges, which helped to eliminate some of mine. Doranne was very helpful with contacts and introductions.

To Nancy Randle of Los Angeles, with her years of experience, serving as an editorial consultant, during my first edit. Thanks to Elizabeth and Catherine of Two Sisters Writing & Publishing for their publishing expertise, hand-holding, and connections to Vangarde Imagery. Thanks Melissa of Shreeve Marketing, for the design and upkeep of my Facebook Author Page.

And finally, without the experience and the folks who were involved in the 1993 and 1996 reenactments in Oregon, I would not have written this book.[1] Many people became best friends. Some, unfortunately, have passed on and will not hear my thanks. Nevertheless, they were inspirational. A very special thanks to three of my friends, now gone: Leslie Wyman, a huge support and talented horse woman; Liz Henderson, a wonderful friend, mule handler, and lady; and Don Roulette, a true gentleman with a penchant for history of the west and ever a staunch supporter of the true historical experiences.

---

1   This book is a work of fiction. The characters, incidents, and dialogue are products of the author's imagination and should not be construed as real. This fictional book was inspired by the true, historical event of The Applegate Trail in 1846.

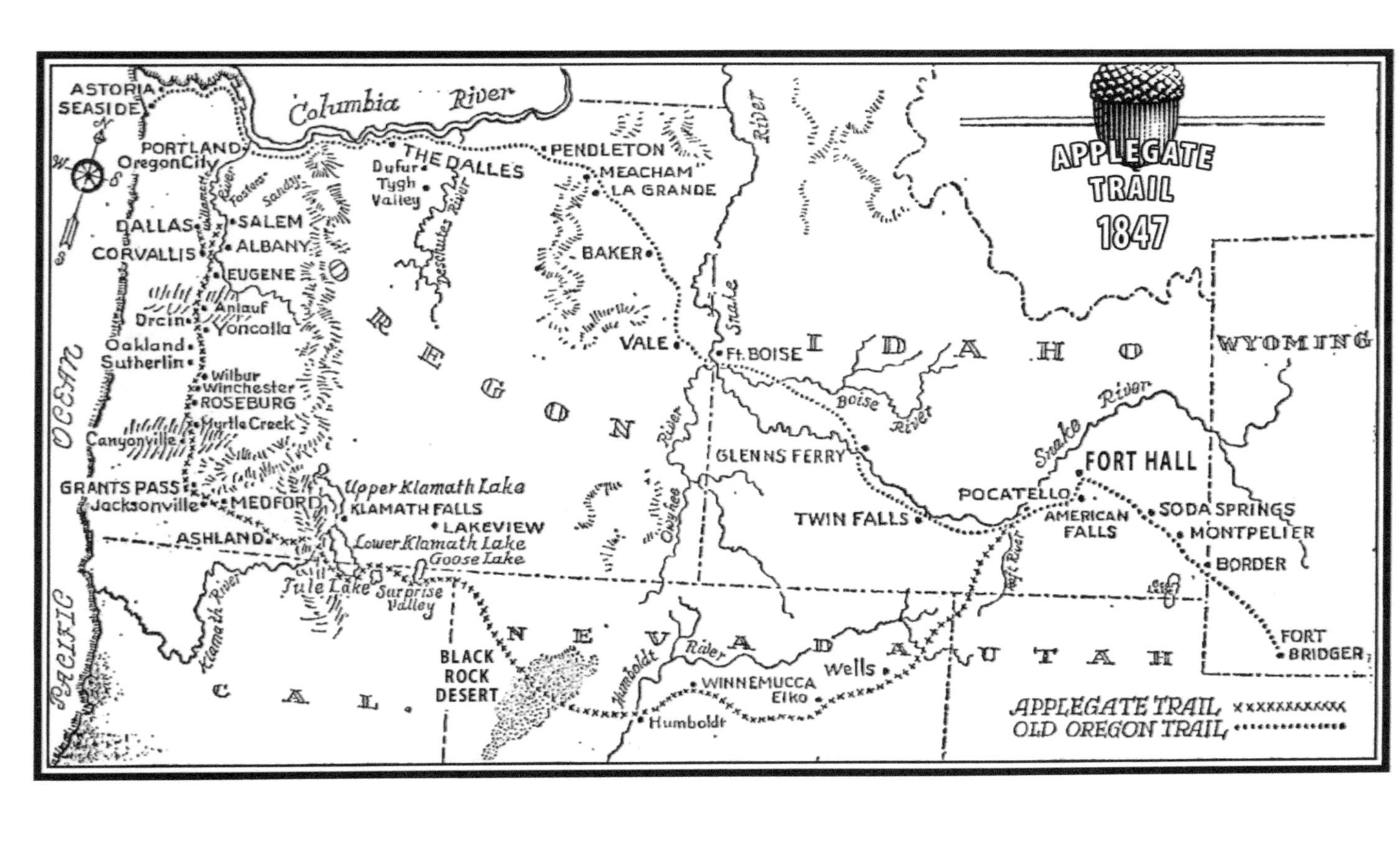

APPLEGATE TRAIL 1847
Columbia River
ASTORIA
SEASIDE
PORTLAND
OregonCity
THE DALLES
PENDLETON
MEACHAM
LA GRANDE
Dufur
Tygh Valley
Deschutes River
DALLAS
SALEM
ALBANY
CORVALLIS
EUGENE
Drain
Anlauf
Yoncalla
Oakland
Sutherlin
Wilbur
Winchester
ROSEBURG
Myrtle Creek
Canyonville
GRANTS PASS
Jacksonville
MEDFORD
ASHLAND
Upper Klamath Lake
KLAMATH FALLS
LAKEVIEW
Lower Klamath Lake
Goose Lake
Tule Lake
Surprise Valley
Klamath River
BAKER
VALE
Snake River
Ft. BOISE
IDAHO
Boise River
GLENNS FERRY
TWIN FALLS
POCATELLO
FORT HALL
AMERICAN FALLS
SODA SPRINGS
MONTPELIER
BORDER
Raft River
FORT BRIDGER
WYOMING
UTAH
NEVADA
CAL.
BLACK ROCK DESERT
Humboldt River
WINNEMUCCA
Elko
Wells
Humboldt
OREGON
OCEAN
PACIFIC
APPLEGATE TRAIL xxxxxxxxxxxx
OLD OREGON TRAIL ....
N W S E

Chapter One

It was hard to think with the sweat coursing down my back and underarms. The Black Rock Desert blazed in the midafternoon sun. My head ached and my eyes burned from tears that had flowed until they were salt streaks down my cheeks, dried up like the desert where I stood alone.

Two days had passed since the wagons had moved on without me and my husband Nalan. When we left Fort Hall, Idaho, it had not seemed like such a hard trip. Excitement had lit my husband's eyes as he told me of his dreams for the Oregon Territory. But our wagon had bogged down in the sand with the extra weight of our household possessions. Possessions that Nalan had insisted we needed. But Nalan would not have to worry about those possessions any longer, for he laid face toward the heavens, scorching, and dead from some horrible malady that the desert had dished out to so many travelers.

We left Fort Hall in the spring of 1847 to follow a trail they called "Applegate." Supposedly it was a safer route that would lead us to green pastures and wide-open spaces with beauty all around us. Water running clear and fish jumping at least six feet. But so far, it had taken everything that I held dear to me. I had left my Mama and Papa back home in Fort Hall, used all our money to buy a wagon and extra provisions, and now I had lost my husband.

Nalan was older than me, as most everyone was. My Papa had said that I needed to marry a more mature man so that I would be taken care of properly. Mama didn't say much, except that I should marry for love and no other reason. Mama wasn't much of a talker, but she was a great listener and a gracious woman, even with her arms buried to the elbow in the weekly wash pan. She made it her life's work to raise me and my brother Elliott to become hard-working and caring adults.

Elliott had married a couple of years before me and had a couple of young'uns. He lived just outside of Fort Hall. I guess he was happy. So when Nalan, who was 15 years older than me, talked to my Pa about courting me, it was fine. He was a decent-looking man, strong and lean. He cared about what people thought of him, but not always about how I felt. So when he decided we were going to the Oregon Territory, I didn't have much to say about it. It didn't matter that I was educated and had an opinion, and that I wanted to share it.

My folks wouldn't leave Fort Hall because they had too many ties there. I think they were hoping that eventually Nalan would get tired of Oregon and bring me home. Well, Nalan wouldn't be taking me anywhere now. The sun continued to scorch the land where I stood for as far as I could see. His body seemed to grow larger, the longer it lay on the hot earth. The buzzards began to gather, and I thought most certainly that they were going to make me wretch with their stingy, bulging eyes and long necks searching the ground below.

I walked to Nalan's body and removed his neckerchief. I carefully shook the dust from it, drained some water from the barrel on the side of the wagon, wrung it out, and lay it flat over his hot, scorched face.

Dear Lord, please don't let that look of anguish on his face haunt me for the remainder of my days.

I approached the wagon, knowing I could not give Nalan's body a proper burial, but instead had to do as others had done along the trail before me: dig a shallow grave, then drive the wagon over it to protect the burial site from being desecrated by wild animals and Indians.

Somehow the people on this trail had continued in the face of hardships, and I had to also do that. I needed to catch up to the other members of the train in order to survive.

After placing Nalan's body in a shallow hole and carefully placing hot sand over it, I moved to the back of my wagon, removed a large water pan, and drained more water from the barrel. I placed it in front of my oxen, Nellie and Locks. Next came one of the largest pieces of furniture in the wagon: a wardrobe built of pine and lined in cedar. My husband had received it as a wedding gift from his folks in Fort Hall. It wasn't a family heirloom, just a gift, because his folks were happy for him.

It took all of my strength mentally as well as physically to push the large piece of furniture to the back edge of the wagon. I had removed Nalan's clothes from the wardrobe and lay them on the ground outside the wagon. Next, I removed my clothing from the wardrobe, folded them neatly, and put them into a chest that had come from home. I tied a rope around the wardrobe, unhooked the oxen, and took them behind the wagon. There I hooked the harness to their yokes, the rope to the furniture, and the oxen pulled the wardrobe out from the back of the wagon. It crashed to the ground, splintering the wood and what was left of the life that I had shared for two years with my husband.

I must survive. I unloaded the night washstand that had stood beside our four-poster bed back home, and lastly the four-poster bedposts. All lay in a pile in the hot sand under the scorching sun.

The oxen, once freshly watered and rested, pulled the wagon easily under the lightened load. I drove the team from high up in the seat now, with a prod to occasionally poke the oxen from behind, no longer walking as I had for most of the trip from Fort Hall. The majority of people had walked the distance due to the heavy loads the wagons carried. It wasn't always very comfortable on the seat, nor was there enough room for the large families that passed by way of the Applegate Trail.

I traveled for a full day before I spotted wagon tracks just before nightfall. After taking care of Nellie and Locks, I was exhausted as I slowly drank a cup of water while checking out the surroundings where I would spend the night. I was unafraid. I figured God was saving me for something. Otherwise, He would have taken me with Nalan. But just in case, I kept a loaded gun and a canteen of water near me that night. I slept in the wagon on a cot with my shoes on and my head out the back of the wagon in case anyone came my way. I was a great one for looking trouble square in the face.

I was 15 when Nalan and I married, so by now that made me 17. Some considered me good-looking. Thick, dark hair with a little wave. Red lips that were shaped pert and eyebrows that naturally arched. Long legs and a nice smile. Mama always said I was very curvy, which made the men look at me. I didn't like it when they stared. I was tall, almost 5'8," with dark brown eyes, except when I was mad; then they would turn green. My Papa's eyes did the same thing.

I wore bloomers with my day dresses, but I preferred to wear my brother's britches when no one was looking. I liked the freedom of moving around. Like turning upside down or bending over. Climbing was easier, too, without my dress wrapping around my legs and tripping me up. But a lady wouldn't be caught in them, and now that I was married, actually widowed, I thought I'd better act like a lady.

Chapter Two

BEFORE DAWN THE NEXT morning, my eyes popped wide open in anticipation of getting on the trail. I felt excited at the prospect of following the tracks and catching up with the others from the train. I knew it was not acceptable for a lone woman to be on the train without a chaperone, but I had no idea when I started this crossing that it would end up like this. I washed the sleep from my face, watered the oxen and made sure they had finished the grass hay from the night before, grabbed a chunk of dried beef and my canteen for myself, and I was ready to go.

The oxen accepted their lightened yolks without much of a problem. I took the makeshift reins, and we lumbered onward towards the next precious day of life and hopefully closer to the dream that lulled so many to sleep.

Just before midday, I stopped along the trail to relieve myself and stretch my cramped body from the hours spent on the bumpy wagon seat. As I squatted next to the wagon and looked in the direction I was following, I saw a filmy haze in the air with the slightest hint of the back-end of a wagon.

Oh thank you, God. Tonight I'll spend in the company of other people.

The oxen walked forward at the same methodical pace. Never slowing or speeding up, but consistently moving. I gained on the train, and I continued later into the day after the others had stopped. I continued until I pulled up behind the last wagon.

Setting my brake, I unhooked the yoke from the harness, placed water in a large bucket for them with a little grass hay, and leaned over to pat Nellie and Locks to thank them for getting me this far. My tired, aching, and dusty body leaned against the wagon. With my eyes closed, I listened to the sounds of people talking and getting ready to bed down for the night. I prayed to thank the good Lord for riding with me.

The wagon in front of me noticed I had come up behind them, after a fashion. They had a pretty good size group of kids with them and the missus was with child. She looked to be several months into her next one. One of the young ones told his Ma and Pa that they weren't the last ones in the line anymore, and now I would be eating their dust.

They came back to introduce themselves and find out where I came from. We talked for a spell. I told them of my troubles. They felt real sorry for me and asked me to supper with them. They had eight kids from two years to 16 years old. Sure was a brood. All they were carrying in their wagon was sleeping blankets, clothes, and food. There was no room for anything else. I told the missus that two of the younger ones could ride in my wagon from now on. They didn't weigh much and would be easier to keep track of. They were much obliged. It seemed to take a load of worry off Mary, the missus. Her man went by the name of Ned. They were Ned and Mary Parker.

I didn't meet the wagon master that first- or even the second day, since it was late, and the Parkers and I were kind of playing catch-up to the remainder of the train. Many wagons would get separated for one reason or another. Most got separated because of weight in the wagons, but also because of breakdowns, small children, or even illness and death.

The Parkers were slowed down because of the little ones walking slower with their little legs. When I took the two youngest into my wagon, that helped the Parkers catch up, and it gave me some much-needed company. It can get mighty lonely out on the desert. I felt as if I were part of a family again. The two young Parkers were no problem and very enjoyable to listen to and watch. They jabbered most of the time, sometimes incoherently. They seemed to speak their own language to each other and were quite content.

By the time the train stopped for a rest around midday, we had caught up to the rest of the train. The last three wagons had actually been traveling side-by-side, crossing the desert that day, rather than one behind the other. I was informed that a total of 20 wagons were together as far as anyone could figure. That did not include the wagon master or the horseback riders; they were referred to as "outriders." Keep in mind that wagons being "together" could mean stretched out for miles. Mary looked absolutely exhausted from all her walking, but her wagon was too heavy with their food, clothing, and bedding to change the circumstances.

I sure liked Mary. She was tired-looking, but you could still tell she was once a very pretty woman before the years of childrearing and rough work had started to tell her age. Her man Ned tried to help her as much as possible, but men just didn't have a feel for how much time and energy that childrearing took out of a woman. Mary never complained, because she wanted to please Ned, and she adored her big family.

The Parkers introduced me to three other wagon drivers during our midday break. One man, Chase, was single without other family members traveling with him. The other two wagons were families, one with two children, and another with five children. The Brahms family had already lost two children along the way.

Once we were rested and watered, it was time to move on. Ned suggested that Mary ride in their wagon for the remainder of the day, and he would walk beside the team. The single driver asked if possibly one of the Parker boys could drive my team, Mary could ride on the Parkers' wagon, and I could ride with him. It seemed to make sense. The other five Parker children were still walking, but of an age that it would not cause a hardship for them, as long as their shoes held out.

Chase was helpful and competent. He was a powerfully-built man, with a large barrel chest and muscular arms and hands. He wore a brown shirt, and a black felt hat pulled down low to cover a big portion of his weathered face. He wore spectacles and had a full beard. I also noticed a gap between his front teeth when he smiled and blood that had run down from his eye and dried on the side of his face.

Chase Gunner was his name, and he was a cowboy. We talked throughout the afternoon and into the evening. I didn't even know men had that many words in them or those kinds of thoughts and opinions. He was sensitive to young and old and knew every sound of his wagon and team. I smiled so much that afternoon that my face actually hurt when we reached camp that night. I think it was the first time I'd seen the desert. Or maybe the lighting was different here. Whatever it was, I felt really glad to be here and alive tonight. *The Lord has been good to me.*

Mary Parker looked better today from resting, so we decided that the driving arrangements should stay the same. Her boy Adam was about 15 or 16 years old, as near as I could figure, and would continue to drive my wagon with the two youngest Parkers on board. Mary would ride with her man, and I would ride with Chase. The wagon master came back to check us out today, or rather to check me out. He knew the Parkers, but had not seen them for some time. He seemed glad that they had caught up and that I had also joined up, but he was not very friendly about me riding with Chase. He seemed kind of odd. One minute smiling at me, and the next scowling at Chase. I would think he'd be happy that we were not holding the rest of the train back.

We traveled about 15 miles today, as near as I could figure, a good far piece. Tonight when we got to our campsite, the wagon master, Brad, had us circle the wagons in a larger circle with the fronts of our wagons pointing towards the middle at an angle. Brad said that was so we could get closer to each wagon and not be so spread out. It was time to have a wagon meeting, anyway, so we could all get acquainted. Dinner was cooked at each wagon with people walking around, some sharing, others staying close to their wagons and families. Brad asked me to join a big group of folks toward the middle of the train. Chase followed along close, not letting me get far from his sight.

The oxen were hobbled instead of being on a highline like the horses. The oxen didn't pose as much of a problem for thieves - Indian or white. They also took less care and ate less, making them perfect for a slow-moving group like ours. Now horses were a different story. They would wander off, eat more, and need more water. Either way, animals needed care before anyone had their meal or went to bed.

In the camp, someone pulled a harmonica out after a little bit of talking, and we sang around the fire for a short bit. After a fashion, I began to yawn, as did others.

"Would you like an escort back to your wagon?" Chase asked. "I'm going that direction."

I said good night to everyone and walked beside him.

Brad was younger than Chase. He dressed in yellow chamois leather chaps and a shirt with a brown felt hat shading his blue eyes. He stood about six feet tall with a stocky build. He had muscular legs and arms that moved smoothly beneath the layer of his clothing. He seemed to retain some sort of control over most of the women in camp. From watching him, I would say it was mostly due to his smile. Although it was infrequent, it was a stopper. When he smiled, it was clear up in his eyes and all the way to his chin. The strange thing was that he seemed immune to his own powers. He was more interested in taking care of his wagons. That suited me fine. Chase was always aware of Brad's whereabouts. They seemed to get along well and have a mutual respect for each other. I think they had traveled together before.

I slept like a log last night, knowing I had the protection of others with me. I dreamt a little of Nalan and even saw his swollen face looking back at me. He seemed to be saying to me, "Go forward." I had no choice now. I had nothing to go back to and nothing to get me there even if I did. But regardless of the images in my head, it was the best night's sleep I'd had for a very long time.

We traveled another 15 miles today. The day went by pleasantly and much faster than the previous days, since I had someone to talk with. Chase was a very easy listener and paid close attention to me. I thought perhaps I would have to be a bit careful or he would get the wrong idea. After all, my husband's grave was not yet firm.

Mary was riding in her wagon and her little ones were riding in my wagon with their older brother. It had not only helped the children, but had taken a strain from her as well. I really liked the Parkers. They were a wonderful family. I surely hoped God did not decide to take any of their children along the trail, as he had many others. Their son Adam was doing a fine job of driving my Nellie and Locks. He was a quiet young man and very pleasant to be around. His younger brothers and sisters seemed to trust that he would always be there for them.

Chapter Three

The springs where we stopped today were very hot. I heard someone refer to it as Cholona Crossing or Double Hot Springs. The ground had a strange white color to it. Everyone's eyes were stinging and turning red and weeping. It didn't seem to cause any irritation other than our eyes. The ground was very hard.

That part concerned Brad more than anything.

"I'm worried that the hot spring is too inviting," he said. "I've heard about places like this caving in." We noticed animal bones around the outside edges of the hot spring and decided—even though we were anxious to bathe—that maybe we should just stay clear of the place. We camped some ways away.

"Don't go near the spring," Brad warned everyone. "I don't want to have to fish anyone out with their meat scalded off their bones, not even good buzzard bait."

Several of us helped each other by sharing our meager dinner fare tonight. It seemed everyone was getting somewhat irritable because of the burning eyes and the lure of the spring, but the unavailability of it. It taunted us after so many weeks of not having a decent bath. I certainly looked forward to a good soak sometime soon, as did everyone else.

I told the Parkers that one of their youngest children could also share my wagon at night with me. Since I had unloaded many provisions, more room for such a small body seemed a small price to pay for the companionship that I had received. The little one was not much into whining, and he sure fell asleep quick in my wagon once out of the wind and off the ground. His parents called him Tom, but his older siblings call him Pain.

"It's 'cause he's a pain in the bottom," his sister said. It didn't sound like they really thought that he was a pain, but they enjoyed teasing him. Adam was always carrying Tom on his back or swinging him around.

Someday, I thought, *when I have young ones.*

Chase had been helping with my team of oxen in the morning and evening and seemed to enjoy working with the animals. He also made a point of explaining everything he did to the wagon or animals. I think it was because he understood that I had no man, and that I needed to be able to take care of my animals by myself. Luckily, my Pa had taught me a bunch as well.

I listened really close to others when they talked about what was right for my oxen team. As I mentioned, Chase had been teaching me, as well as helping me and had made me feel like a pampered woman, but one who could actually think. He was real good company, too.

"I had planned to come on the Applegate Trail with my soon-to-be new wife," he told me. "Well, one week before the train left out of Fort Hall, she up and took off with some other fellow. She was a comfortable age and easy to look at, but not nearly as pretty or as kind as you've been."

I smiled, then he continued. "I'm not sure she would have made it, anyway. She was pretty spoiled and probably would have complained a whole lot."

I think he tried to make light of the situation, but it truly did hurt him inside something bad. *Well, I must say, after meeting Chase and traveling with him, she was a foolish woman, and her loss is my good fortune.*

Brad came back to sit with us a short spell tonight.

"So far, it's been easy crossing," he said, "but soon we'll come to some tough mountain crossings. Places where we'll have to clear the trees to get our wagons over the mountains. There'll come days when we'll be darn lucky to make five miles or even less. Be extra careful each night with checking your wagons and stock. We need everything in good working order and everyone fully aware of what will be happening."

Brad continued by telling me that the Parker boy could lead my team over some of those mountains.

"But you'll be responsible for most of it," he said, "since all the menfolk will be expected to be on the end of a rope holding wagons down mountains."

"I'm not here for a handout," I told him, "and I'll do whatever I have to do to keep my wagon on the road and do my share with the group."

Chase told the two of us that he would help out however he could with anyone who needed extra help. He also made mention to Brad that so far I was doing better than most, since I already had the sense to lighten my load. It was announced, at that point, that the little guys should walk going down these mountains instead of riding, so as not to take a chance on ending up at the bottom of a ravine with splintered wood as their untimely gravesites.

After Brad left the fire, Chase asked me to walk with him and make a final night check of the oxen. I think he just wanted to see me safely to my wagon so I wouldn't trip or get sidetracked by some lonely man traveling on the train. So far, I had had nothing to be concerned about since all the men I had met had been gentlemen. Of course, Chase was never far from my side. It was such a comfort.

I tucked little Tom into my wagon for a night's sleep before I bedded down. It was nice having a little person so near. Listening to quiet voices in the dark, the night sounds of animals, and the soft noise coming from this sweet young-un, it didn't take me long to fall into a peaceful slumber. I could only imagine what crossing these mountains would be like. Though I was always one for looking danger in the eye, I sure could have used a few more of these nice, calm days.

Chapter Four

BRAD WARNED US LAST night that it would be pretty warm to-day, similar to an Indian summer before the cold weather started in. I was not sure what that meant, but he seemed to think it was good. We were up and ready to roll at daybreak.

I prepared some warm mush for Chase, little Tom, and myself before hitting the trail today. Put some jerked beef and fruit that Mama had dried in a small drawstring bag and refilled our canteens from the water barrel, in case we got separated from them.

"I'm the lucky one," Chase commented later that morning. "I feel guilty to get so much attention at the expense of your husband's passing."

"You don't have anything to feel guilty about," I said, "since you had nothing to do with my husband's passing or staying."

He smiled, grateful as we chewed our jerked beef and savored the dried fruit as the day passed.

Well, I guess it had to happen, since everything has been going so smoothly after joining this group of good folks.

The mountains really were beautiful—from a distance. Up close, those big pine trees and underbrush were so thick, there was no way a horse was getting through by itself, let alone this group of wagons.

"Hold up for a bit to make some preparations for what's ahead," Brad ordered. We all unhooked our teams and gave them some water and a little dry hay as we rested them through the midday. The women prepared some dry meals out of the backs of the wagons that we could have that evening, since camp would be set up pronto and perhaps not all of us would be at one site.

The menfolk, including the very young men, took off on foot or horseback with axes, scythes, and ropes to see about clearing trees and brush or moving some of the bigger obstacles. Chase and Brad told all the women before leaving to "load your rifles and be ready to fire first and ask questions later."

Everyone seemed to be more afraid of the Indians than I was. Maybe that was because I hadn't had any run-ins with them. We loaded our rifles anyway and kept them close for the day, just as Brad and Chase had said to do. Mary Parker and a few of the other women who were expecting laid down for a short rest in the early afternoon. Even though the rest was short, Mary said it renewed her strength and would enable her to continue in much better spirits. Mr. Parker was very lucky to have her.

I mixed a batch of biscuits and put them in the Dutch oven over a small fire between a ring of rocks. Figured they would taste mighty good with some of that jerked beef.

About three in the afternoon, the menfolk got back looking sweaty and tired, but insisting that we must at least get all the wagons to the top of the hill in order to camp that evening. This would allow us the entire day tomorrow, if needed, to lower our wagons and supplies down the other side. They felt that the clearing they had done was adequate for the wagons to pass through, but the descent was too steep to attempt in the dusk or without support from ropes. Even though it was quite warm and the air was still, the mountainside allowed ample shade on this side for us to feel comfortable.

No one was riding up the hillside. Everyone, including Mary Parker and her children, was walking, with many of them pushing on the sides of a wagon and helping to take some weight from the non-complaining oxen. By dark, all 20 wagons were at the top of the short hill climb. The wagons were not circled, but instead parked wherever they could find a space large and flat enough to park and bed down for the night. The oxen were tied to trees, never to a wagon, for fear they would move and pull a wagon over a cliff. Wagon owners made sure to chock their wheels. We were all exhausted. It was good that the women planned cold meals for the evening, because many were too tired to eat. Besides, we had inadequate room to prepare a meal without the danger of causing a fire.

Our traveling companions were helpful. However, there was always an exception to the rule. That was in the form of one man. Rush Spencer. He caused considerable discomfort to everyone, especially Brad. He constantly reminded us that his way was the best and the only way. He also seemed to think it was acceptable to flirt outrageously with the women on the train. I wondered what a man was thinking in these kinds of circumstances. His needs must certainly have been as basic as an animal, given his rude behavior.

"She's unavailable to you or any other man on this train," Chase told Mr. Spencer.

Brad backed Chase up and told him: "All the women are unavailable to you on this trip. Now use some of your ornery behavior to help us climb the hills and cross the deserts, instead of complaining and pestering the womenfolk!"

Mr. Spencer was not at all happy. He looked to me as if he were thinking up something to get even with Chase and Brad later on. It made me pretty uncomfortable. I didn't think Chase and Brad were the type of men that Mr. Spencer had better bother much, even though they had both been perfect gentleman.

Chase held my hand for a brief time tonight when he told me to get a good night's sleep, 'cause I was sure going to need it tomorrow.

"But don't forget to also keep an ear open in case Mr. Spencer decided to pay you a visit," he said, adding with a soft pat on the arm, that "another one of those bags of jerked beef and fruit might come in real handy tomorrow." In addition, he told me that, "If there's anything that you could carry that you hold very dear, you might want to take it out of your wagon before we start the wagons down the hillside tomorrow."

I didn't tell him I had made biscuits to go with that jerked beef. *Tomorrow he'll find out.*

Chapter Five

BRAD WOKE EVERYONE THIS morning.

"I want to wish everyone Godspeed by starting the day off with the Lord's blessing," he said. "Mr. Whittacker said he'd be proud to talk to the Lord on our behalf."

As we bowed our heads in prayer, little Tom Parker quietly slipped his hand into mine. The smile of sheer innocence and faith on that little face was all I needed to feel strong for whatever the day brought us. If that weren't enough, when I handed Chase a soft biscuit with some of my blackberry preserves on it, his face told me how grateful he was.

The first wagon was brought forward and unhitched, with a rope tied to the rear axle of the wagon and to a strong tree. All the menfolk, except for the wagon owner, got on the end of the rope and began to lower the wagon, hand over hand, down the hillside. Mr. Gill, the wagon owner of that first wagon, was in front, guiding the hitch to steer the wagon through the trees to its safety at the bottom of the hill. Mrs. Gill had taken the team of oxen and led them down the hill and out of the way in case the wagon should break loose. The wagon was safely lowered, as were the next three wagons.

On the fourth wagon, loaded heavily with family furniture and possessions, Brad asked the Rosses to unload some of their belongings. The menfolk did not want the added weight on the tree or their arms as they held the wagon back. Mrs. Ross began to cry that she couldn't leave any of her family's belongings behind. Brad told the Rosses that if the rope broke, then Mr. Ross would quite likely be run over by the wagon, and the wagon would be in several pieces, as would her possessions. Brad asked them, "Wouldn't you rather unload beforehand?"

"I'm sure everything will work out fine," Mr. Ross said. "I don't want to upset my new wife or to make her do without the things that made her happy in the wilderness."

The Ross' wagon almost made it. It was lowered within 50 feet from the bottom of the hillside before one wheel hung up on a dislodged rock. Mr. Ross left the tongue of the wagon and began trying to move the rock, with the help of his nephew who had previously been helping with the weight on the rope. Luckily for Mr. Ross, he was not holding the tongue in front of the wagon when it literally leapt from the hands of the men trying to control its descent.

"Get back!" Brad yelled at Mr. Ross and his nephew. He yelled for anyone at the bottom of the hill to move out of the way of the wagon. Men tried to catch the end of the rope tied to the careening wagon as it plummeted to the bottom of the hill, smashing into trees and branches on the way down.

No one was hurt, if you didn't count Mrs. Ross' feelings and broken heart. But the wagon was splintered and lay in thousands of shreds at the bottom of the hill. This would be only one of the testimonies and reminders of the harshness of the trip out west.

After searching the hillside, Mr. and Mrs. Ross salvaged their clothing and a couple of family books, including her family Bible, but all of their prized furniture and most food staples littered the side of the hill and acted as a memento for others to follow.

Brad's mouth was set in a firm line from that point forward. He was unyielding.

"I'll be the one to make the decision on the weight," he said. "If I say articles need to be removed before letting the wagon down, things will be removed. Anyone who argues will be asked to leave the train and finish on your own. Is that clear?"

By that time, everyone, especially the Rosses, were in agreement and gave no argument. The rest of the wagons were lowered without incident.

By the time we had lowered all the wagons, now numbering 19, to the bottom of the hill, an entire day had passed. It was late afternoon and too late to make much mileage and everyone was too tired. Adam and the young ones had taken the three teams of oxen down the hill and staked them out to graze. They had brought Chase's team, mine, and of course their own team.

Mary and the children had gathered small branches and sticks for the evening's cook fires. But no one felt up to cooking tonight because of the hard day. It was a great thing that we had small, dry meals already prepared. Mrs. Gill, being the first wagon down the hill, had put a huge pot of dried beans on to cook that morning. They sure smelled wonderful. She was more than happy to share as long as they lasted. I added my biscuits to our fare until they were gone. We all felt pretty contented.

Everyone was happy to hit the bedroll that night. The only rested living things in camp were the oxen and the horses. They had grazed all day and were quite relaxed. That was good, because we had another hill, although smaller, to tackle tomorrow. Chase and Brad seemed to think we could get up and over in one day and would have much less clearing to do. We would be able to drive the wagons to the top with everyone pushing on them.

After a good night's rest and knowing that we could go anywhere as long as everyone worked together, spirits were high. Mary Parker worried me, though, because of her aches and severe tiredness. I guessed that was normal, but since I had never birthed a child, I had no experience to compare it to. She tried hard to keep a constant smile and comforting words for her children and her man, but it seemed to me a person would have to be blind to not see how tired she looked. She said this morning she didn't feel she was doing her share during the day so she was going to start soaking a pot of beans at night and through the next day so we could at least have a hot meal at night when we got to camp. I had made a silent vow to do everything I could to help her do that.

Chapter Six

WE LOADED THE WAGONS after a short breakfast of fried bacon with dry, cold biscuits and molasses poured over them. After hooking up the wagons, we pulled out and headed for the mountain. Brad, the wagon master, did a funny thing this morning. Without any discussion, he told the Parkers to move their wagon into the number two position; Chase would be number three, and my wagon would be number four. It was not uncommon to switch wagon positions on a train, but usually there was some discussion with the teamsters first.

The first wagon—with everyone pushing or pulling, except for Mary Parker and her three smallest children, Chase, myself, and Adam Parker, who was driving my wagon—was up and over the hill in no time. Next went the Parkers' wagon.

Mary didn't ride because of the added weight and danger. I walked beside her, helping her manage the children, as we climbed the small hill up and over, always staying to the side and slightly behind the wagon in case it should break loose and become a runaway. We did not unhook the oxen going down this hill. Brad did not feel that the hill was steep enough or long enough to cause that much strain on our oxen.

Everyone, besides those I mentioned, did hold the ropes on

each wagon in case there were any problems. The drivers walked beside the wagon with a tug line to keep the oxen calm and slow going down the hill. Without someone aboard the wagon to hold the brake, the oxen would bear the full weight of the wagons on their backsides without our help.

When we got to the bottom with the Parkers' wagon, I immediately saw the relief on Mary's face. We had Mr. Parker lead the team out of the way, as did Chase and Adam with the next two wagons.

About that time, Brad showed up on his saddle horse that was usually tied behind his wagon when he wasn't driving his team.

"Don't get comfortable yet, folks," he said. "Chase, I'd like for you to take these first four wagons and keep moving. Mrs. Parker, you ride with your man, in position number two. Chase, move your wagon into number one position and travel another seven or eight miles today before you stop. Unless it gets too rough or brushy, then of course stop the wagons. Mrs. Nalan, you drive your own team today, so Adam can walk behind the last wagon and keep a look-out for the next wagon coming from the hill. Everybody stay within sight distance of each other in case of trouble."

I guess my mouth was hanging open, because Brad said, "You got questions, Mrs. Nalan?"

"No, Brad, I don't have questions."

"Are you not wanting to drive your wagon, ma'am?" he asked.

"No Brad, that's not a problem. I drove it all the way here from my husband's grave on the desert. I'm not afraid."

"Well what is that look on your face, if I may ask?"

I thought for a moment more before answering, "Well Brad, you surprised me with the name you called me; it's my own fault. I guess I never took the time to tell anyone my name. It's not Mrs. Nalan."

By this time everyone was just staring at me, waiting to hear my first name. I don't know how I had ever forgotten to mention it before. I guess it didn't seem necessary. A thought went through my head: *at this time, I can choose any name I want, and no one would ever be the wiser.*

"My name is Questa," I said.

At first, there was dead silence.

"I apologize for never asking your name," Mary said.

Then Chase spoke: "Well, I think that is one of the purtiest names I've ever heard. But it goes real well with one of the purtiest ladies I've ever seen." Then he dipped the front of his hat to me and nodded to Brad that everything was in order. Brad smiled at me, dipped his hat, turned his horse, and rode away toward the hill and the other 15 wagons creeping one by one down the hillside.

Chase moved his wagon into number one position, after hoisting one of the Parker youngsters up on the seat with him. Mr. Gill told me to go after the Parkers; he would bring up the rear. Adam would walk behind his wagon and in front of the wagons coming down the hillside. I thanked him and put the other two Parker youngsters in my wagon to save their young legs.

The oxen were able to travel at a steady speed for the next three hours, covering about six miles. Chase told everyone to stop and take a break, do nature's bidding, or water up. He thought it a good idea if everyone got off the seats and stretched real good, too. It would also give him a chance to run back to Adam to find out if the other wagons had caught up yet. While he was doing that, we gave a bit of water to our oxen as all of us watered, stretched, and visited the bushes for a little sorely missed privacy.

The ground was fairly level, and Chase was finding a good route, missing brushy areas, so we hadn't had to cut brush and do clearing. That was why we were moving along at such a steady pace. I thought our outriders, along with the wagon master, were doing a great job scouting. Mary Parker checked her bean pot while we stopped to make sure they still had water in them. She also pulled out a strap of fat bacon and put it in the bean pot. She said it would be for flavoring when we finally stopped and cooked for the evening.

Chase got back and said the wagons were all pretty well catching us or at the very least in good sight. He advised us to mount up or walk and to get rolling again. He figured we would travel for another hour before stopping. That was exciting for the women trying to prepare meals, since we had to find fuel for the fire. It was always nice to do that in the daylight. Besides, everyone knew that beans took a while to cook.

True to his word, Chase halted the train about an hour down the trail. We had a small mountain range to the east of us, and to our backs, the hillside we had just come over. A small creek, with a very nice clear hole of water, neighbored us that evening. Chase told us to leave a good wide gap between the water source and any trails that led to it for the critters that might feel inclined to show up during the night.

It could not have been a better place to overnight if we had tried. Chase suggested we load up on water for our wagons, which we all did. The very first thing I did was to help Mary gather wood and start the fire for the pot of beans. Once that was done, we set about having the children gather more wood for the fires tonight.

I rigged up a clothesline, with the help of Mary and her oldest daughter, who was 12. We put the line between two trees. I then gathered my dirty laundry and went to the watering hole next to a big rock. I mentioned to Mary's daughter Trish that it would be nice if she could do the laundry for her Mother and give her a rest. I offered to help.

Trish and I worked side by side on the rock. First soaping our clothes with a bar of lye soap, then rubbing them against the rock and dipping them back in the water. The water was cold, but since it was still light out, the young Parker children were bathing in the ice-cold dampness. They took turns with the bar of soap, running it over each other's heads and shoulders, the older children doing most of the chore for the youngsters. Squeals of delight and chattering teeth accented the late afternoon as the children finished their cleansing rituals. By the time they had finished bathing, Trish and I had finished our laundry.

It occurred to me at that point that Chase probably had a need for a few clean items. I hung my laundry and helped Trish hang her family's laundry before I told her that I would stand watch over the hole of water if she would like to bathe. But first I was going to ask Mr. Gunner if I could help him with his laundry needs. Chase just looked at me with a dumbfounded look on his face. I wiped my chin.

"Is my face dirty?" I asked. "Or am I drooling like a fool?"

"No Ma'am, you sure ain't no fool," he said. "I just never had a woman offer to do my laundry before, unless it was my Ma or I was paying for it."

I smiled at Chase and told him to give me two or three items that he would be needing to wear soon, and I would do my best to get them cleaned and dried tonight. I also told Chase that I did have my price. I wanted him to keep all the menfolk and children away from the water hole for the next hour, until dark, so the women could bathe. After dark, the men could have a turn. He smiled and said he would be delighted to grant me that wish and hoped we would enjoy the house facilities.

Chapter Seven

Mary Parker, Mrs. Gill, and I went to the watering hole. They bathed while I washed one pair of britches, one shirt, and one pair of long-handled underwear for Chase, which I promised not to get embarrassed about when I laundered. I finished with the laundry about the time that the two women were finishing their ritual. They went back to camp and offered to hang the wet laundry while I finished my bathing.

I gratefully accepted as I lowered myself, in my underdrawers, into the icy water. I soaped my hair and my body as best I could before submerging again. I decided a swim was in order, since I was already wet to the skin. The water was cold, but still offered comfort and solitude that I had been sorely missing. It was quiet with just me in the water. I could barely hear the voices of the group up on the trail camp and just caught a wisp of campfire smoke as I imagined it simmering the pot of beans that Mary had been so protective over. I heard a grunt and the large bush on the bank moved as I quietly reflected the trip and the friendships that I hoped would last forever.

My feet found their way to the sandy bottom of the watering hole. I cleared the water out of my eyes and looked toward the bush and the noise. There on the bank of the watering hole, which was, as Brad had suggested, a watering hole for other life forms long before we arrived, stood a very large black bear. The bear on all fours seemed to be confused about the smells surrounding his favorite watering spot. There were no deer or fish for him to swat, and what was that odd smell?

I think the human scent was totally foreign to him. Thankfully he had not spotted me yet, but I knew without a doubt that once he discovered me, it would only take him a few seconds to get to me—who had no weapons—in the water. I had to get out and alert the camp without disturbing the bear into charging.

As I slowly began to move toward the bank, my attention focused on something else moving. Rush Spencer had been in the bushes watching me as I bathed and floated around. He had removed his shirt and shoes and looked as if he were planning on joining me in my bath, even though I had certainly not requested his company. He had stopped dead in his tracks, though, when he noticed the big black bear on the other side of the watering hole. He held his finger over his lips as if to say, "Don't make a sound," as he backed up the bank and toward the camp.

I was frozen in the water from fear. I was oblivious to the icy temperatures of the water. Turning my head slowly, I looked over my shoulder to check the bear's whereabouts. He still was on the bank, but was sniffing the air and turning closer to my direction. I wondered what Rush Spencer was doing. Was he getting a gun or help, or just trying to cover his whereabouts, since I had spotted him eyeballing me? Whatever he was doing, I sure hoped it was going to be quick, because the bear was now squarely facing me and giving me a real sick feeling in my stomach that he had spotted me and thought I was dinner, or at the very least an intruder.

The bear let out a huge roar, tossing his head to one side. He leapt forward toward the water. I figured I'd better be quick or there would be absolutely no chance of survival. I headed for the bank, feeling so sluggish in the water. As I got to the bank and started to climb out, I heard a shout above my head. I looked up while still scampering up the bank. There stood Chase Gunner with a rifle raised and pointed at the big black bear. Next to him, Mr. Gill also had his rifle raised, and running up behind was Mr. Parker swinging into action. "Down, woman!" Chase yelled.

I hit the bank of dry sand on my stomach just in time for Chase to fire the first blast at the bear. He hit it, but it only slowed the bear as Mr. Gill's gun fired and missed the bear. Chase had reloaded and fired again as I felt the hot breath of the bear on the back of my calves. The bear went down, dead as it hit the ground. "You got him, Chase!" Mr. Parker shouted. "That was some good shootin'!" I was stunned. I couldn't move. In only moments, Chase was beside me, picking me up while wrapping both arms around me and speaking real soft-like.

"Everything will be fine now," he said, "Chase won't let anything hurt you." I looked at him with tears of relief mirrored in my face. At that point, I knew that Nalan had done me a huge favor. I pulled myself up with Chase's help, shuddered, recognized my immodest attire and told him we should dress the bear and tan the hides. He looked stunned. But only for a minute, before he showed amusement and disbelief, but smiled and agreed as he gave me a hand to stand on my own two feet.

Adam, Rush, Mr. Gill, and Brad, who had just gotten there, picked up the bear, with all four of them carrying as well as dragging the huge animal up the bank toward the camp where they began rigging it up in the trees to dress the bear out.

"Would you mind standing there on the riverbank for a few minutes with your back turned to me?" I asked Chase. I wanted to rinse the sand off myself and my underclothes before drying off, but I didn't want any more uninvited company. He nodded and turned his back.

After I had gotten my clothes on, Chase and I walked toward the camp, stopping at the site where the rigging was with the bear hanging. We talked with the others, who had the young Parker boys start another fire ring close to the bear hanging. They were using it for added light, since evening was approaching. They would also use it to begin smoking the meat and to keep other animals away from camp tonight. Adam, Brad, and Mr. Gill would sleep with their rifles ready, close to our new meal source tonight. Our wagons were parked close together with the oxen grazing on the inside of the circle.

After checking with Mary to see how her beans were progressing, I went to my wagon and began mixing biscuits. I pulled butter and a couple of potatoes from my stored goods. Washed and sliced the potatoes into a frying pan with a couple of cut-up green onions. I moved the frying pan away from the fire so as not to cook too fast, put the big black iron lid on and walked to the line where our clothes were drying.

My clothes that I had washed earlier were doing pretty good, but Chase's clothes were still pretty damp. I knew they weren't going to get any drier tonight with the dampness. I pulled a big tarp out of my wagon and Trish offered to help me rig it up. I removed enough clothes from the line to drape the tarp over the line. The tarp reached the ground on one side where, with Trish's help, I anchored each corner. The portion of tarp that hung over the top of the line, I stretched from each corner to the front and back of my wagon bows with short pieces of rope. I now had a waterproof lean-to.

The children were gathering by this time and were excited because they figured it was their sleeping arrangements. I told them if they could find a place where there were no dripping-wet clothes, they were welcome to it. I then ran another line between two tripods under the waterproof tarp and re-hung the wettest clothing items.

I had the Parker children bring me more wood and rocks, and we rigged a smaller fire ring just outside the tarp with the wind blowing the smoke and warmth from the fire through the lean-to. The clothes would smell a little like campfire smoke, but they would be warm in the morning and so would the children.

Brad came along checking everything a little later. He liked my rigging and suggested we might put that arrangement up every night when possible to accommodate dry sleeping. Without wet laundry hanging, even more people could stay dry. Chase smiled at me and nodded his approval.

"Beans are ready!" Mary yelled. My biscuits were done in the Dutch oven—and with butter, a few fried potatoes, and blackberry sauce from Mrs. Gill—the Parker family, the Gills, Chase, and I felt like royalty. Clean laundry, clean bodies, dry sleeping place, and hot food. We couldn't ask for more than that. After dinner, we all helped with cleaning up as Mary put on another pot of beans with fat backstrap, for tomorrow's meal.

It became a habit of sorts, with the four wagons sticking close together and watching after each other. We ate many meals together and talked with each other in the evening. There wasn't much time during the day with all of us spread out and the wagons being kind of noisy and all. But we had a fine time in the evening, even as tired as everyone was.

Brad was often joining us in the evening during his rounds. We would ask him to sit for dinner with us. He got where after a spell he would only stay for dinner if he could contribute something to the meal. Many times it was fruit, berries, or vegetables that he had dried or picked along the trail. They were a great complement to the meal.

Two days after the kill of the bear at the watering hole, the menfolk asked me: "What do you want done with your bear?"

Well, firstly, I didn't figure it was *my* bear, but since they said it was, I wanted to share the meat with everyone.

Brad had said we were due to stop the next day for a rest of a couple of days. There were trees, a watering hole, and lots of grazing grass for the oxen.

"I'd like to have a group trail cook," I said. "Make a couple of big pots of bear stew with everyone adding something to the pots." Because there were nigh on 80 people on the train, we would need six stewpots with everyone contributing to their group stew. The camping area was large enough for all the wagons to circle, so Brad actually had six circles of wagons with each having its own community-share pot.

The excitement that night was wonderful. Two or three campfires in each group blazed, with the largest fire in the middle holding their camp pot of bear stew. Each member brought something for the pot or added to the meal with biscuits, apple butter, fresh berries or another item to share. It was a great time to meet others and talk about the trip and how they ended up on such a quest. There were lots of young ones on the trail and more than a few women due to deliver along the way. They looked as tired as Mary Parker or worse.

Dinner was barely done in most of the six camps when musical instruments started to appear. Someone had a juice harp, a couple of fiddles showed up, and along came a guitar. One young man had a pipe that had the most calming sounds coming from it. He said he had bought it from some trapper before leaving Fort Hall. Probably had been owned by some savage. The thought crossed my mind that it was not the type of instrument that a savage would play. It was the kind of sound that comes from a meadowlark on an early morning or the sound of spring when it first wakes. No, whoever owned it, whoever had designed it, was not a savage, not in my mind at least.

First one couple and a few of the children started to dance to the music, and then others joined in. Until finally all the married folks were waltzing, even the more pregnant women were enjoying the pleasure of the waltz. I smiled as I watched and dreamed about a time more than two years ago when I waltzed the last time. It wasn't with Nalan. He didn't dance. He didn't fun around either. When I married him, I married old commitment and no tomfoolery.

I felt the slightest touch on my shoulder. I turned and found Chase very close to me with a sweet smile asking for this dance. He came around in front of me. Swept his hat off and bowed low as he held his right hand out, waiting for me to accept his offer. I was delighted and stepped into his arms like I had been born there. Around the hard dirt he waltzed me. Never stepping on my toes, like many young men had done years before.

He held me not too tight, but tight enough where I could feel the heat from his body and smell his masculine scent. He smelled like oxen and sweat and bear stew, none of which was a bad smell. It was real and a scent that I could live with. We danced many more dances after that, mostly slow ones, always keeping a respect-ful distance.

Chase hardly allowed anyone else close to me. Although, young Adam Parker was allowed a dance with me, and afterwards Chase told me that the young man was quite taken with me. I asked him how he figured that.

"He's a man," Chase said, "although young, and no man can resist you if he's got a brain or a lick of sense."

The night was just what we all needed, and most especially me.

When the music finally stopped and folks started back to their camp, I decided to help the Parker children get bedrolls squarely under the tarp in case of dampness. I also wanted to see how the small campfire ring was doing beside the tarp.

We were planning to do laundry early tomorrow, since it was a rest day, and get our clothes hung early in the day so they would dry and not hang under the tarp, dripping all night. I wasn't paying much attention as I started around the back of my wagon toward the tarp and the trees, when I felt a hand clasp tightly over my mouth from behind.

I knew right away it had to be someone from the camp, since I could smell the grain alcohol on his breath. He jerked me back against his body tight and sort of ground his privates up against me to let me know he had himself a true hankering to get familiar with me. I wasn't scared, but I sure was mad. I was mad that I had worked as hard on this trip as any man, and I still had to put up with these no-account brutes demoralizing me like this. I was mad cause this was ruining my evening. An evening I was treasuring. Now he was going to ruin it for me with an experience I had no desire for. I was so mad I believe my eyes had turned green.

"Be real quiet," he ordered.

I bit down on his fingers as hard as I could.

At the same time, I raised my foot and jumped down hard on his foot with my hard-soled boots.

He yelped and shoved me to the ground as he held one foot with his good hand and did a jingle of a dance on his other foot.

If I knew for sure I had cured him, I would have laughed, but I wasn't sure that he wouldn't regain his strength and come after me to get even for my rough behavior. *Well,* I figured, *I have nothing to lose now, so I may as well finish the job on this no-good coyote.*

So, I jumped up and grabbed a sturdy limb of soon-to-be firewood and whacked him soundly on his shin. He fell to the ground and rolled around, holding on to his shin first, then his foot, then sucking on his hand that still had my teeth marks. *Well, that ought to take care of him for tonight anyway,* I thought, *but what about tomorrow?* It was Rush Spencer, and the varmint had already sneaked up on me twice.

I stomped away to finish what I had started by checking on the Parker children and the fire ring. Becoming much more aware of the sounds of pests than I had been earlier. I found some of the children already curled up and fast asleep under the tarp's overhead cover. Tom was in the back of my wagon in his regular spot. Mary Parker, Trish, and Adam were checking the fire, and Adam piled a few more branches close to his bedroll so he could easily feed the fire during the night. He smiled at me and thanked me again for the tarp's protection and the dance. I started cautiously back around my wagon when I heard the sound of flesh hitting flesh and grunts of indistinguishable origin. I inched toward the sounds, making sure to keep my presence a secret. What I saw will forever be etched in my mind.

Chase Gunner was giving Rush Spencer the beating of his life. He would only stop long enough for Rush to get back on his feet before he resumed his onslaught again. The entire time he never said a word. Other men, including Brad, stood by and watched in silence. No one interfered or said a word. There were no women-folk around. Rush Spencer was a strong man, and not small by any standards, but he probably had been a bully most of his life. He was getting his comeuppance, and Chase Gunner was just the man to do it. He was making sure that Spencer would not be bullying anyone else, at least not on this wagon train.

After the deed was done and all were silent, Chase squatted beside Spencer and in a voice so quiet you had to hold your breath to hear it, he issued a warning: "Spencer, if you ever lay your hands, your eyes, or any other part of your no-good body on Questa, or any other woman, child, or man in this camp again, I will person-ally kill you."

Then Brad spoke. "Stay with your wagon, Spencer, and don't go near that young woman again or I will take care of you myself."

And they strode away with the other men.

Chapter Eight

THE NEXT MORNING, OUR resting day dawned sunny but cold. Everyone looked happy. Chase's hands, particularly his right knuckles, were swollen, but he was uncomplaining.

Mary Parker, our group of women from the six wagons, and I had a brief discussion and decided to have a group breakfast over three fires. Mary filled the large black skillet with slices of ham that she had been saving, while Mrs. Gill started the biscuits in her Dutch oven. Adam had picked wild onions and some wild sage earlier. I sliced potatoes into my skillet over the third fire and started the potatoes, onions, and sage with lots of strong black pepper and a little bear grease. The women from another wagon had fixed a massive pot of coffee, and they had a couple of goats to add milk for the coffee. The hickory coffee and bacon and onions were enough to make anyone's mouth water.

Chase was working on the wagons, as were misters Gill and Parker, while the women prepared breakfast. Mary had asked Adam to gather more branches with the young'uns and string another line for clothes-washing today. Brad came by, carrying special salve that he said worked real good on sores for the oxen, and people, too. He dabbed a bit on the necks of the oxen with little Tom Parker following close on his heels, jabbering nonstop, as if a magpie.

Breakfast was ready. Brad stopped and ate with us before moving down the line with the salve. After breakfast was cleared up, Mary put her pot of beans over the central fire ring and started to prepare for washing laundry. I told Mary that Trish and I could handle what laundry needs her family had. Adam showed up and said he wouldn't mind helping do laundry since he helped dirty it. Shortly after he showed up, Chase came by and asked if there was room for him to spread his laundry out too. *I wonder about these menfolk. Never have I been around such a helpful bunch.*

Chase started to work on his laundry; I noticed him wincing when he tried to scrub his clothing with the lye soap all over his hands. His knuckles were swollen and red by the time I realized why he was wincing. They must have burned something powerful. I carefully took the clothes from Chase's hands.

"I just don't think there's enough room for all of us to be working our laundry," I told him, "but I can do yours if you can put some of that good oxen salve around the feet of my oxen, too. I noticed they had some pretty bad rock scars around their feet. I don't want them to get sore and not be able to pull my wagon."

Chase looked a little sorry at first, then he looked at me with a smile as he placed his one, not-so-swollen hand on the top of my wrist and said, "You're one heck of a woman. Questa."

For the remainder of the day, everyone worked on their wagons while the women and children gathered berries, wild onion, or any other edible plant life we could identify. We had a trapper on the trail by the Indian name of "he who throws a long shadow." We called him Dennis. He identified plants that some of us were totally unfamiliar with, and we replenished our food additives and medicine bags. Dennis also knew a lot about hides and how to cure them. He spent a little time with Chase, showing him how to finish curing my bear hide and not waste any part. He also spent time showing Trish how to weave baskets from vines and grass. Adam followed him around in the afternoon, then asked if he could go with him to scout ahead for the travel route for the next few days. Mary was a bit worried, but Brad assured her that if anybody could teach him and take care of him, it was Dennis.

Dennis and Adam showed up late in camp that night with good and bad news. They said that the next three days of travel would be good and fairly easy travel, making about 10 to 12 miles a day. It was the fourth day that would be our challenge. They had traveled to a large river crossing. Dennis said on day three, we would need to stay an extra day to prepare for the crossing.

As Dennis and Adam had promised, the next three traveling days went well and were uneventful. We made an average of 12 miles per day and all of us had developed our own chores, which created a rhythm that we could all get along with.

Trish continued to walk and weave baskets as Dennis had shown her. She even braided some wood-carrying lines that the young children could use to carry more than one or two sticks when gathering wood. The one item that she asked Dennis to help her with was the strongest choice of fiber to weave a basket for the baby that her Mother would deliver along the trail. I cherished the memory of this thoughtful bunch of travelers, but most of all, I cherished Mary Parker and her children, besides Chase, of course.

On the third night, we camped beside a mighty river. Brad reminded us, even though some of us did not need reminding, to allow animals their natural trail to the river for watering. He also said, with a slight grin, that venison stew would taste great for a meal or two. Brad, Dennis, and Chase began setting a trap for any unsuspecting animal that would visit the watering spot that night. Dennis set a trap in the river made of reeds of long grass. He anchored it to a small tree at the shoreline so the current would not take it downstream. With any luck, we could add fish to our menu soon.

Adam went off into the trees a little bit from camp and seemed busy. He came back after a bit and asked his sister Trish, to bring a couple of slender, long branches from the fire ring and her strongest woven wood-carrying line. She packed off into the brush with him, and they talked quietly and seemed to work very well together. After their job was done, I noticed Adam sweeping the ground with a branch and carefully laying it down. I asked them what they had done. Adam said they had set a trap to catch small animals such as a rabbit. A friend had shown him how to set the trap, but it was his first attempt. He was very excited, as was his sister.

I sure hope that of all the traps that have been set around camp tonight, I thought, *at least Adam catches something edible.* This land that we are crossing was abundant in every way. More hills, woods, fish, and four-legged creatures than we had dreamed of.

Brad was able to circle the wagons in groups of six, as we did in one other campsite where we feasted on bear stew. Since we would be here tomorrow preparing for our river crossing, we needed ample room and the help of everyone in camp.

The next morning, very early, Chase was up before dawn with my bear hide stretched tight between two trees. Dennis was talking with him as he scraped with a strange-looking, sharp object.

"Chase will fix you a warm bear hide for your wagon seat or teepee—your choice," Dennis said. I didn't know if he was kidding.

As the women started breakfast, the men met in the middle of the circle of wagons with Brad to talk about their plans for the river crossing tomorrow. Dennis had been told to hit the trail and be back before dark to explain the crossing location to Brad and the others. In the meantime, the camp looked as busy as an anthill.

A bucket of linseed oil came out of the Parkers' wagon, and Mr. Parker told Adam to start with their wagon, then Questa's wagon, then Chase's wagon, and so on.

"Paint the linseed oil on the sideboards up high, good and thick," Mr. Parker said. "Don't put it on the undercarriage or the first few sideboards."

They were melting paraffin in a large metal pot to cover the bottoms and sideboards of the wagons. As it melted, the men replaced the hardened paraffin and began using a flat, thin board to place the hot wax on the seams of the wagon's bottom and lower sideboards.

Chase and Mr. Gill, with grease bucket in hand, were a wagon ahead, re-greasing the wheels and making sure of their road-worthiness. After all the wagon bottoms in our group of six were sealed with paraffin, the men moved to the next camp to make sure there had been enough of the sealant to go around in each camp.

Everyone was well-prepared on account of the list of supplies that Brad had supplied them with at Fort Hall. Trish was able to eke out a little leftover paraffin that she used on the bottom of her baskets. She said it was to keep them from absorbing the water. Even though she was not finished with the babe's cradle, she also treated the bottom portion with the paraffin. I could plainly see she was a sensible girl who gave considerable thought to detail and to her family's needs.

The menfolk also checked all the wagon brakes: a block of wood attached to a hand lever that when pulled connected to the wagon wheel, putting pressure on the wheel to slow or stop the wagon, depending on the pressure applied. When the blocks of wood became worn or pitted, they were ineffective.

By daybreak that day, Adam had a grin on his face bigger than all outdoors. He had caught a very nice rabbit in his new creation. Trish was as proud of her part in the catch as he was. He immediately set the trap again, since it was, as he said, "another day." Our fish traps were empty, but only because a smarter animal had found our catch and taken it before we got to it. Brad did manage to shoot a nice deer at daybreak. *Looks like venison stew tonight.* "I can have a nice skin, too, brain-tanned," Brad said, "and make good use of the antlers for buttons for my new buckskin britches I'll make from the deerskin."

Mary had continued soaking a pot of beans each day and getting adequate rest this past month of the trip. But she continued to get more tired and larger with the added weight. I didn't believe that she could carry that child much longer. But Ned, that was Mister Parker, had also been keeping a close eye on Mary. He was not an unobservant man; he knew what a prize he had in her.

Most of the morning, Brad had Rocky and another buckaroo using the oxen to pull logs up to camp. I met Rocky and Ben, both handsome men, fine with animals, especially broncs, and hard workers, at the Bear Camp where we danced. *I think I'll call it that from now on:* the Bear Camp, where we ate the bear stew, danced, and convened.

Brad, Adam, Chase, and Mr. Gill had already started binding logs together to make a makeshift boat, more of a raft, actually. "We're not sure if we'll find a shallow crossing to drive across or have to load our wagons on the rafts and float them," Brad said, adding, "We must be prepared either way. We'll know when Dennis returns what the verdict is: to float or drive across the river crossing."

Once the logs were lashed together tightly for a base, Brad had four more logs brought to each raft. There were six rafts total, one for each group. Two of the logs were attached on top of the raft running sideways so the wagons would not slip sideways. In addition, these logs were for those pushing the raft across the river to have a place to station their feet. On the front of each raft, a shorter log was placed and tied down to act as a stop for the wheels. It was lashed tightly to the raft base. The fourth log would be placed on each raft tomorrow as each wagon was floated, if need be.

It seemed like a lot of work, but Brad said even if we didn't use them this time, it would be great practice for all of us for the next river, and he promised there would be others. Regardless, the wagons were in better and more watertight condition if we had to cross on the power of the wagons without the benefit of the rafts.

Chapter Nine

THE NEXT MORNING, EVERYONE looked a little tired from fretting all night about what was ahead. It had helped a little to know before hitting the bedrolls that we would actually be using the rafts to cross. On the other hand, that meant the water was deep and swift, too deep and swift to cross with the wagons on their own power.

Brad, Chase, and Misters Gill and Parker seemed to be the brains behind most of what was happening. Dennis knew all about the crossing points in the river from his scouting expedition the day before. He told Brad that the wagons needed to be evenly weighted on both sides, as well as on the front and back. The raft could not, he said, make a distinction of which end was supposed to go first once it starts across the river. Wagons should be tied down well to the rafts to prevent shifting.

The oxen would be expected to swim across unfettered. Any loose articles that we wished to carry with us would not be tied to our bodies in case we were thrown from the raft. Folks would ride over on a separate raft and wait on the other side for our lives to arrive in the form of a wagon and four-legged animals.

One by one, the wagons pulled forward and lined up to cross the river. The anticipation of the crossing was deafening. Each family member held others close as if this were possibly their last time together.

"Pull your wagon up," Brad told Mr. Gill. Chase had gone to the other side of the river to man a rope that he had pulled across and anchored solidly to a stout tree on the opposite bank. The goal was to give him enough leverage to help keep the wagon on a straight course. Three other men had crossed on single horses as well, so as to give assistance. They had pushed the bank of the river down in a couple of areas where they hoped to "land" the rafts and unload the wagons, allowing lots of room for the oxen once they were hooked back to the wagons and could pull them from the river.

The work would have to be quick once the raft reached the shore. They did not want the raft to start twisting around and risk being tipped over, especially with the few passengers that were sharing the raft floating their wagon.

As Mr. Gill pulled his wagon up as far as possible before unhooking the oxen, all the menfolk were there to lend a hand. It went quickly and oh-so-quietly. This was a serious business, moving our lives across this roiling river.

Oxen were stationed near the edge, close enough to move them over and tantalize them to continue across the river once they were unhooked from their wagon. They swam to the other side with the direction of horsemen and trudged solidly and slowly up the other bank. They were stopped in a holding stance at the edge of the bank, ready to pull the wagon off the raft once it arrived. All lines were ready.

Ten men pushed at Brad's command. The Gills' wagon rolled up and onto the raft. At least four men tied down the wagon to the raft, making sure that it was weighted correctly on the anchored float. Once all was aboard and everything felt and looked satisfactory, Brad gave the order for it to begin its trip across. Brad had decided that with this first raft, he preferred that only Mr. Gill be on board; no missus or children were allowed. "It's a maiden voyage that may have some kinks in it yet," he said.

But with a rope across the river to help guide the raft and Mr. Gill using a long pole to help keep the raft on course, it did just that. It floated straight to the other side and pulled up, just like it was intended. Quickly, Brad was down to the raft and helping to hook the oxen up. In no time, they were signaled to pull and the wagon rolled off the raft and up the bank to safety.

I didn't realize until that moment that I had been holding my breath the entire morning, and apparently so had everyone else. A huge sigh escaped my lips as slaps on the legs with hats, clapping, and smiles spread across the river banks—both of them.

Mr. Gill was now helping on the opposite side of the river, at least until it was time to go back and help his own family cross.

A second wagon and a third wagon were brought forward, loaded and tied down, and ferried safely across the river. Only they carried passengers as well. Never more than four, though. We didn't want too many children to have to cross without an adult, just in case. Brad said that families were lost that way, and he didn't want that burden hanging on his shoulders.

When it came time for my wagon, Chase was instantly by my side. "Are you comfortable with this?" he asked in a low and easy voice.

"I'm a bit scared," I said, "but I can and will do it, just like everyone else had managed." I also assured him that he could put a couple of others on the raft with me. It made no sense to not use my crossing for some of those that were waiting. One of Mr. Gill's family members got on board with me and two of the darling

Parker children came aboard with total trust in their young faces. *"Oh Lord,"* I prayed, *"please keep us safe."*

And He delivered us. He guided us right to the opposite shore. Me, with the long stick in my hands, helping as much as an earthly being could have done. Between the rope to guide us, a stick for keeping us moving, and those darling children being very still and quiet—all was uneventful, unless you considered the part of holding my breath. My oxen waited on the opposite bank, swishing their backsides very calmly, much more calmly than I felt, that much I was certain of. Looking back at Chase, I thought he would burst at our safe arrival. I knew from his face that he had also held his breath.

Many more oxen moved forward and swam their lethargic, heavy bodies across the wide expanse with relatively no problems. When it came down to the last three pairs of oxen and the last three wagons, things got a bit crazy. The Lindes, whom I had not met, pulled their team of oxen up to the side of the river, very loudly declaring that they should not have been one of the last three wagons to cross the river.

Chase assured them that everyone had a turn, and that was the way the barrel had turned for them. He asked Mr. Linde if he had taken all the precautions with the linseed oil and checked the paraffin to make sure the raft was somewhat waterproof. Mr. Linde regarded Chase as if it were none of his concern, and he wasn't wasting his breath on an answer. Chase was much more tolerant of the man than I think I could have been. He kept a silent tongue.

Mr. Linde insisted the oxen could cross on their own without a horse guiding them, and quickly and soundly whacked the bovines on the backside. They nearly jumped into the river, as fast as an ox could jump that is, and began to swim. However, when he scared them into the river, they entered crooked and were crossing each other. From there on, it was trouble. They were practically swimming over the tops of each other and not making much headway except for going downstream. Both teams bellowed and fought the water. Mr. Linde yelled at them, which only added to the fray.

Once again, Chase and Brad were ever-ready. Chase quickly mounted his horse from the west bank of the river while Brad was on his on the east side. Both headed down the bank going downstream after the oxen. The wagons could not afford to lose any oxen; we had no extras. If the oxen were lost, then the Lindes' possessions would have been lost too. No one else had extra room for the weight of the Lindes' household.

After about a half hour of thrashing in the water and swimming the horses pretty hard, Chase and Brad rescued one of the oxen, but not the other. Once they returned with it, they took it to the east bank to wait for the arrival of the Lindes' wagon. They also brought another team of the oxen from the east side of the bank to help pull the wagon off the raft once it arrived. The fate of the Linde wagon was yet to be determined.

Chapter Ten

The remainder of the wagons and the oxen came across without a problem. For those, Chase Gunner tied his horse to a rope and had someone gently nudge him in the direction of the bank. He had no problems. After the Lindes' upset, the rest of the families kept their tongues about them. No one else yelled or cursed or threw fits as Mr. Linde had. Everyone was quiet while waiting for Brad to give the Lindes his decision.

Once the wagons and the oxen were all across, other family members that were unable to travel across with their wagons were loaded onto the rafts, no more than 10 to a raft, and brought across. Families were broken up for the crossing. In case a raft were to tip over, an entire family would not be lost. It went very smoothly, and everyone was very cooperative and still. The rafts served their purpose, and we had made our first major crossing. *Amen.*

The mood in camp that night was one of mixed feelings. We all knew that the Lindes were probably going to get served some pretty sour news, but we also were so relieved to have made the crossings and lost no human lives. The ox would have made it had Linde not spooked it into the water. Whatever ration was served up, he most assuredly deserved, although Mrs. Linde certainly didn't. Living with the mister would have been bad punishment enough for any woman.

Everyone pitched in once again amongst our six or so wagons, and we had a splendid dinner served right along with the mood. The Parkers, Gills, Chase, Brad, myself, and two other wagons joined us for our community meal.

Immediately following our dinner, Brad called a meeting of all of us traveling in the wagons. He said he wanted each of us to have a say and not be shy about it. And then whatever decision was reached regarding the Lindes loss of an oxen, he wanted us to forget about it and get a good night's sleep.

Brad told us what the Lindes had in their wagon and what the one ox could pull. Nothing but the wagon and food stores. First, he asked if anyone of us had room in our wagons for anything extra that belonged to the Lindes. Then he told all of us, straight in our faces: "Don't feel obliged or guilty if you can't." No one had extra room. In fact, most of us had already thrown out prized possessions all across the desert to keep our stock rolling and healthy.

Brad and Chase agreed that the one ox would be hard-pressed to pull the wagon by itself and keep up. None of us wanted the train slowed down because of a mistake by Mr. Linde that could have been avoided. He put all of us in jeopardy with his angry temper and lack of forethought. The final consensus was that the Lindes would be moved to the back of the train. They both would have to walk to save their oxen. It would pull the wagon as best it could. Mr. Linde was very angry once again, but kept his mouth still for a change. Tears silently slipped down Mrs. Linde's worn face, but she never uttered a sound.

That night, the water ran by us and left us to our sleep. The night critters came around and drank and probably eyed us wearily, but were silent. Deer prints dotted the banks come morning, and our fish trap boasted of a good, fresh catch for breakfast. What a treat, all served up with sliced potatoes and wild onions. This land got richer, the further west we traveled. The wildlife, the soil, even the sky seemed bigger.

Maybe it's true what they said about the territory of Oregon, I thought. *If that' so, I certainly look forward to what's ahead and actually reaching that Eden at the end of the trail. If there really is an end.*

We were a little slow-moving this morning. Brad let us lag a bit on purpose. He had sent Dennis ahead once again to get the lay of the land and the water. Adam went with him, so I had time to drive my own wagon for a spell. That was fine, except that I wouldn't be sitting with Chase. I would, however, have the company of the delightful Parker children. Adam was learning so much from Dennis; he was blossoming. Speak of blossoming, Mary Parker looked like she had bloomed in full color. Her condition became more pronounced as the hours went by. I guessed that after so many children, this one would not overstay its welcome. I was predicting she would have it earlier than what she had originally planned.

One of the Parker children, little Jeremiah, decided to go relieve himself before the wagons set out. He was five and quite the little explorer.

"He's been gone for some time," Mary said.

"I'll go look for him," I said, since she was slowed by her discomfort.

"Please call out to him," she said, "since he may be a bit embarrassed if you walk up on him."

I went in the direction of a spit of bank that had some reeds and a few small trees around it.

"Jeremiah!" I hollered softly at first, then louder, as I did not get an answer right away. And then I saw why.

Jeremiah was squatted down on the ground in fear. His little eyes could not be pulled away from the reeds, where a mountain lion had come down for a drink. The large cat sat crouched within pouncing distance of the small boy and stared him square in the eyes. I was sure the feline saw breakfast and was aware that vittles looked him in the face.

I could barely croak out in a whisper to Jeremiah to be very still and not move, and then I prayed. *God, if you're in this part of the country, please come to our aid as soon as possible. Be it in the form of someone with a very large gun that was a good shot or a giant hailstorm or possibly a huge elk that the feline might enjoy more.*

Once again, the sweat started to form on my skin, and I could tell that it would soon start to carry the smell of fear with it.

Jeremiah was frozen and was not likely to say anything or be able to move. I had to believe that the cat's attention was still on Jeremiah, probably because he was smaller and more attainable. Either way, I sensed more than heard the movement behind me. I knew that Chase was there. I prayed that Chase was there.

A small stone landed just to the right and a bit behind the cat. The cat lunged to his right to catch an unsuspecting prey, and when he did, the shot blasted into the early morning. There was not a second shot; thank goodness that was not necessary. Chase's shot rang true and square and the large cat lay dead not more than two feet from where he sat watching little Jeremiah.

Jeremiah fell flat on the ground in a large sigh, and tears rolled down the young'un's smooth cheeks. Dirt caked onto his face, but the look of pure terror was easing the longer he lay there. He knew that Chase had killed the animal, and he would be seeing his Ma and Pa another day.

I looked at Chase with wonder and shook my head as I got to my feet and ran to Jeremiah to gather him in my arms. Chase was beside me with his arm protectively touching my back. He let out a huge sigh as well, seeing that both Jeremiah and I were all right. He took Jeremiah from my arms and carried him back to camp, along with his gun in the other arm.

Camp folks heard the shot and came running. Ned Parker was the first to make it there and took Jeremiah in his arms as he covered him with kisses that blended with the tears running down his own cheeks. As Chase and I explained what had happened, a couple of the menfolk went back to the river to gather the cat. He would be good eating.

Jeremiah stayed close to his folks that morning, and everyone else was somewhat reluctant to get too far from camp. We established a new rule that no one was to venture from camp again for any reason, unless someone was with them and carrying a loaded and "ready to fire" gun.

I pulled on Chase's sleeve as we got closer to camp.

"I need to say something," I said. He left the talking to me. As we rounded my wagon, and got free of prying eyes, I could not help myself. I looked up at Chase and threw my arms around his neck as I laid my head against his broad, strong chest. I thanked him from the bottom of my heart.

"Chase, I don't know how you were brought into my life, but I know I would not have a life if it weren't for you. You are always there for me. You seem to know when I need you and that seems to be for most of this trip."

Chase put his arms around me protectively and said, "Sh-sh, Darlin'. It's my pleasure and my joy to be able to help you, and I absolutely thank the Creator for pickin' me for this job. Now, how about we get ourselves ready for the new day."

With that, a slow, slight squeeze of my body next to him and my arms still around his neck, he took my hand in his and off we went.

Chapter Eleven

THE DAY WAS BRIGHT with promise. We had survived once again, and the small assembly became even closer. I prayed that when we got to our Eden in the Oregon Territory, that we would find places that were close to each other. I so cherished these new friends and thought they were the type of neighbors I could really enjoy living near for the remainder of my days.

Having said that, I didn't know what my life would be like when we reached our destination, because Nalan never shared much with me about Oregon or what it was like. I heard tell from some of the folks on the trail that it was lush, with fish jumping and plenty of game for eating, and good dirt to grow in and wide-open spaces to raise our young'uns. *I'm not afraid, and I'm trusting that this is right, and that the good Lord will provide and take care of me. He has thus far.*

Everyone took their same places on the train, except for the Lindes, who are now at the back of the train, and we traveled over the next several days without much change. We averaged about 13 miles a day, gathering at night with our six-wagon traveling groups for our meals. Little Jeremiah and the rest of the children, and adults too, learned a good lesson about straying away from camp after that morning on the river with the big cat.

Speaking of the cat. I'd never had cat meat before, but it wasn't bad, fixed in a stew. Dennis was pretty handy with the skin. He called it a "pelt" and was making something out of it. Besides being tall and lanky and a man of few words, he was also pretty secretive about what the pelt's purpose was.

Mary Parker started having some signs this morning of an early delivery. She was riding in the wagon instead of walking, with the word from Brad that in case she needed assistance, the other misses and myself were to stay close to the Parker wagon while traveling.

We were following the riverbank pretty close and had extra water and provisions, so Brad said that when her time was here, we would stop and greet the newest Parker family member in true family fashion. I guessed that meant we would take a break from the trail long enough to deliver her young'un and make her as comfortable as possible. In the meantime, we needed to keep moving.

I asked Adam Parker today what he thought Oregon was going to be. He, being so young and all, had little to say, but you knew that what he said he had given a lot of thought to. Adam told me what his Pa and Ma had said:

"It meant a new life for them with their own piece of fertile land and wide-open spaces to roam. It was abundant with fish and wildlife, and, most importantly, there were others, just like the Parkers, that wanted to have freedom from the east and its over-crowded cities."

I could tell he was excited, even though he also expressed that he knew it was still untamed and wild, and we would all be pioneers to the land's settlement. Just maybe, that was a big part of its draw.

I kept thinking about the end of the Trail. And, of course, talking about it only brought more questions to my head. *How will I know the right place to settle? How will I build myself a home? How will I make a living? Does Chase Gunner really care for me as a woman?* So many questions. *I guess the good Lord is the only with one with the answers, and He's not showing His cards quite yet. He has taken care of me this far, so I guess that will just have to do for now.*

About six hours down the trail, Mary Parker started her labor of the newest addition to our traveling family. Brad rode back to my wagon and asked me to let Adam drive my team so I could go ahead up to Mary and see if I couldn't help to make her more comfortable. I moved right away, even though I hadn't helped to birth any babes. My Ma always did that, and I would assist her, but we always had a doc handy, too, since we lived in town and all. But I got into the wagon, and started preparing rags and getting things close to me that I might need.

Brad said for me to give him a holler when the time got real close, and he would bring Mrs. Brahm back and stop the train. Mrs. Brahm evidently had delivered or assisted in birthing before and was willing to help. This made me feel a whole lot better, since Mary was quite early with this delivery. She was very large, and we figured she was mistaken about her delivery date, and all the walking had hurried the babe along.

But nature is much smarter than we are. An hour after I got into the wagon with Mary, things were getting pretty fast, and the movement of the wagon, although fairly smooth at that point, was very disturbing to Mary and causing her much discomfort. She was full into her labor.

"Stop!" I called out to Brad. "Get Mrs. Brahm back here, pronto! Somebody get a fire started and water heated, and be quick about it!"

"It's time!" Mary told me. I'm pretty sure she knew more than we did since she'd birthed many young'uns prior to this one.

Mrs. Brahm arrived in time to have me wash up and help her tuck coverings under Mary to keep her comfortable and dry. At the same time, we had a small cover ready for the new arrival. We had a cutting utensil and small, clean rags next to a large pan of water.

There was lots of activity outside the wagon as well. A lean-to was being erected on both sides of the wagon, mostly to help keep the sun directly off the sides of the wagon canvas in order to keep Mary and the babe from getting overheated. It would also enable the entire family to sleep under the lean-to tonight and keep the family close.

The time was finally here. Mary began to push after about quarter an hour. As she pushed, I watched with total awe and amazement of the sight before me. The smallest head peaked out with lots of dark hair, and then with another movement, shoulders pressed their way into the world. It was a very tiny boy, and he was fighting for his air and staking his own claim to this Oregon Territory.

Mary was mumbling and still very uncomfortable. Mrs. Brahm and I were working quickly to clean the babe, and get his cord and everything taken care of. We carefully wiped his tiny mouth and then started to lay him on his Ma's breast.

"I need to push again!" Mary yelled. We laid the newborn over on the blanket to attend to the completion of his Ma's delivery.

You could imagine our surprise when we prepared to take care of completing the delivery, but instead saw another of the tiniest heads peak out of her Ma. Mary was having another babe.

She had been carrying twins and didn't know it. This was the tiniest child I had ever seen, and she had the most beautiful, delicate features as well. She reminded me of a glass doll I had once received as a gift from my grandmother. She was precious and so very quiet. She lay still and limp in Mrs. Brahms' hands.

We both looked at each other, then Mrs. Brahm went into action. She started to gently massage the babe on her small chest and back. Ever-so-gently with two fingers, she continued. At the same time, I took a tiny, wet rag and swabbed out her small mouth as Mrs. Brahm once again turned her over. Mary lay still, watching with terror in her face as we did what little we could to get a breath from the wee little girl.

With tears in her eyes, Mary eventually took the little girl and laid her on her breast on her side. She gently kissed the top of her head and spoke to her with words of love that only a mother could express.

"Margaret," Mary called her. It was such a proper name for such a small babe. The wee one shuddered, sighed, and was quiet again and for always.

Mrs. Brahm and I almost forgot ourselves, but realized we had a young man to take care of, along with completing the delivery and cleanup of Mary. We needed to make her as comfortable as could be expected under the circumstances. I took the little boy, who was by now making us aware that even though he was little, he was mighty. His little fists were beginning to rotate as he curled his little lips back and let loose with a determined "notice me" cry. Mary asked for him and as we placed him in her arms, we gently removed Margaret.

Mary gave us permission with her eyes and a slight nod of her head. I wrapped the perfect little girl in a small blanket and held her in my arms.

Oh Lord, why does something so perfect not get a chance in this world? Is this just one of the many perils of crossing the Trail? I know this has happened to many before us, but how do these people manage to continue on?

By the time we had finished with the cleanup, Mary had her young son contently purring in her arms. His little eyes opened as mere slits as he studied his Mother and suckled on his bottom lip. "I'll call him Nikolus James Parker," Mary said. "Please bring Ned to me and give us some time."

We left the wagon. Ned waited outside on a log with his other children sitting around him. When he saw us leave the wagon, he was quickly to his feet with a smile of expectation. He had, after all, heard the cries of his young son.

Mrs. Brahm and I went to him and told him his wife would like to see him. We would stay with the children. We took the youngest children by the hands and asked the older ones to help us find some firewood for tonight's meal. They were, as always, very willing.

Upon our return to the camp, I had a brief moment to speak with Chase and explained to him what had happened. I spoke to no one else, since I was not sure how Ned and Mary wanted to handle it with the others. I knew Chase would not say anything to anyone. He suggested that we get the camp set up and let the Parkers have their time. We would be there if they needed us. I guessed that was all anyone could ask for in this life, to have friends there when you needed them, and of course the good Lord holding your hand.

That afternoon, we had probably gathered enough firewood to last us the next three or four days. That was good, because we never knew what type of terrain we would have from day to day. We still had meat from the cat, which was once again a great community stew. With some wild onions, meat, a little flour for thickener, and each of the six wagons adding something, the stew grew to a fine robust pot of flavors with great smells that made your mouth water.

I didn't realize how hungry I had gotten during the day, having been kept pretty busy with Mary and her birthing. If I were this hungry, she must have been starving.

Ned had come out of the wagon while we gathered wood. With the help of Mr. Brahm, he had dug a grave for little Margaret. He had picked a spot not too close to the river to be washed out, but close enough that the soil was not hard, and it could be dug deep. He said he didn't want everyone in the train to be aware of what had happened, but he did want our six wagons along with the Brahms to give his little girl a proper burial and send-off.

Late that afternoon, little Margaret was carried by her father in the small reed basket that her older sister had made and placed in a deep gravesite at a beautiful and peaceful place along the trail. Branches were swished over the site many times once the burial was completed, and everyone had had a chance to say their goodbyes, either to themselves or aloud. Mostly it was done to ourselves. That was the way.

This loss was unfortunately part of the circle of life, and these rugged and wonderful folks all understood that. We were all living with some type of loss as we traveled to another life. Mary was at the burial, too. Ned had helped his wife, the mother of his children, to climb from the wagon. She stood silently with her new son in her arms, a slight smile on her face, and so many tears.

The mood in the camp was mixed with the sadness of the burial of Margaret, but also the mood of congratulations for the arrival of young Nikolus. He was small, but he was a charmer. Cooing and reaching out with his tiny fists. Mary could not help but smile. The other Parker children were already staking dibs on who would hold him first.

Stew was served up along with some cold biscuits, and things got pretty quiet. It was as hard a day as it would have been if we had been climbing a mountain. We were all ragged.

Chapter Twelve

We were up the next morning at dawn as everyone bustled around camp, taking care of their daily chores and preparing to hit the trail. Yesterday Brad had said we could take a day of rest for Mary, but she insisted that she would be all right and did not want to hold up the group.

"Today will be a short day," Brad mentioned to me and Chase. "One of the oxen on the Brahm wagon seems a bit poorly this morning. He's not eating like he should, nor did he take enough water. We will be leaving late and stopping early in order to save the animal. That, of course, will also give a shorter day for Mary to be bumped around in the wagon with little Nikolus."

The ox was treated with great care this morning. Mr. Brahm took extra time in feeding, watering, and even giving a rubdown to the animal. He seemed to respond well and put his back into pulling once we had again started down the road. We traveled slower than usual that day.

That made the Lindes happy, since they only had one ox themselves. They were always at the end of the trail, so were the last to arrive at night and usually showed lots of wear and tear from eating everyone's dust.

By the time they would reach camp each night, everyone else would have dinner prepared or well on its way. Mrs. Linde was really showing the signs of the trip and the stress of wondering what would happen when we reached the next mountain range. Brad was keeping tabs on them, but mostly Mrs. Linde, I thought, just because she was a gentle person who happened to be in a tough spot, married to Mr. Linde.

The day passed by without incident, except for the Lindes falling further behind as the day progressed. Both of them were walking. The distance caught up with everyone. By mid-afternoon, Brad could no longer spot them. Mary was feeling pretty uncomfortable as well. Brad had Dennis ride ahead of the train a bit. Once Dennis came back, we traveled for another half hour, and Brad called the train to a halt for the evening. We had actually traveled a pretty good piece today, even with our late start. Dennis had located a pretty nice place for us to camp for the evening.

The wagons were somewhat in a straight line, but with the brush being a bit thicker, it was hard for us to park in a straight line and even harder to make a circle, which we didn't really do that often anyway.

Dennis and Adam immediately went to the river and set some traps. They hoped that they might have a fresh catch before dinner. Mary immediately climbed out of the wagon and asked her husband to take her to the river to freshen up. Adam took the Parker's team of oxen and brushed them while they cooled down. Once a little time had passed, he watered them and gave them some grass and a small amount of oats to chew on. Trish was holding little Nikolas and standing just outside the back of the wagon. Nikolas seemed quite content and was alert with his little eyes searching his sister's lovely young face.

The kettles started to rattle, and folks were finding safe places to build a campfire to prepare the evening's meal. Each day brought new challenges. In our current location, we had much more vegetation. Without the wide-open desert areas, we had to be even more careful of causing fires and also needed to be aware of wild animals and Indians, although we had yet to have a run-in with the Indians.

The fire pits were limited to three tonight for the entire train. So everyone shared their cooking fire and many prepared meals together. That was what I liked about this wagon train. Everyone shared and worked together. Of course, there were always exceptions, like Rush Spencer. But for the most part, everyone got along pretty well.

A lovely young lady came up to our fire tonight and asked to borrow a little bit of flour. She said only a cup-full was all her Ma needed to finish her biscuits. She had gotten low and miscalculated for the meal. Her name was Emily, and she was 15 years old. She was a girl not too tall or too short. In fact, her forehead came about even with Adam's chin. I know this because Adam was staring at her while standing not a foot from her. Come to think of it, Adam and Emily looked like a matched set as she stared back at him. She had dusky-colored eyes, spoke with a little drawl of an accent, and had the prettiest, honey-colored hair and smooth skin.

I took my time getting her some flour and plainly asked Adam to walk Emily back to her wagon. I was certain that I saw Adam give me a look of thanks and a slight smile as he walked away with Emily.

The Brahms' oxen were faring pretty well compared to this morning. But Mr. Brahm rubbed them down again tonight and spent some time with the feeding and watering of them. No one wanted to lose an animal, especially since we were getting closer to some mighty big mountains. I heard that the area that we were within days of was very steep and thick with tall trees and brush. Brad mentioned a place called the Jenny Creek Slide. We had already done some steep mountains, but this one would require lowering wagons by ropes, as well as clearing some of the brush and large rocks.

Brad rode out to the back of the train to check on the Lindes, since there was still no sign of them a couple of hours after the train had stopped. Within half an hour, he was back, leading his horse with Mrs. Linde sitting astride the animal. The horse was piled with a tarp, a bag of flour, and some other food items, as well as a bag with clothes and blankets. He helped Mrs. Linde off his horse and asked the Brahms if she could share their fire and get her dinner started. Mr. Linde was still another hour away, with only one ox pulling their wagon.

Adam Parker helped Mrs. Linde set up a makeshift camp where their wagon would be. She looked exhausted. Adam brought her some water from their wagon, and I offered a kettle that she could use to begin her dinner. She was very appreciative and sighed heavily once she had her food preparations completed and sat down on a log next to her camp.

As Brad had predicted, Mr. Linde rolled into camp with his one oxen and wagon about an hour after Mrs. Linde arrived. He was very tired and quiet. Mr. Linde had had a lot of time to think today with his time away from the other travelers.

After unhooking his single ox, he rubbed the animal down and checked him carefully for any signs of wear from the yoke and harness. Satisfied that the animal was as good as could be expected, he watered and fed him. I noticed that he also put some salve around the bottom of the oxen's feet to keep them from getting sore on the rocks or uneven ground. There was certainly a difference in the way he cared for his animal now that he only had one left. It appeared that losing one had made quite an impression. By the time he finished caring for his lone ox, their dinner was done. Mrs. Linde getting in earlier had helped with the timing of their meal.

Mr. and Mrs. Linde moved away from the campfire and walked toward the river. It was good to see that he had been listening to all the warnings and was carrying his rifle with him. They were gone for a short time before returning to their wagon.

Mrs. Linde then climbed in, and within a very short time, a couple of large, heavy kettles were handed out the back to Mr. Linde and set at the base of a tree a few feet from the wagon, but out of the path of travel. Next was a small nightstand, substantially built and heavy looking.

These items were followed by a water basin, pitcher, platter, and a couple of heavy brass candlesticks. Then Mr. Linde climbed out and began to pull a large trunk from the back. Brad and Mr. Brahm happened to be witnessing this and promptly lent a hand to Mr. Linde.

"My wife and I decided these were items that we could live without," Mr. Linde announced, "and we'll be leaving them behind in order to lighten our load. If anyone wants them, you're welcome to take them, but I cannot allow those items to slow them down any further, especially with what's ahead."

Lots of heads were shaking in agreement, but no one said anything. However, Brad did pat Mr. Linde on the back to show a sign of respect for their decision. Hopefully this would enable the Lindes to keep up with the remainder of the wagons from here on out.

Before retiring to my wagon that night, I carefully picked up the washbasin, pitcher, and platter. I didn't feel the weight would slow me down. With it wrapped nicely in a blanket, I was sure it would not be broken and might come in handy somewhere down the trail.

Chapter Thirteen

WE ALL TRAVELED THE next three days, forming a pattern of sorts. Our lineup stayed the same. The Lindes continued to bring up the rear of the train, but they were not so late getting in each night, since they had lightened their wagonload. Mrs. Linde looked a bit more relaxed as well. That could have also been because toward the end of each afternoon, Brad would collect some of her dinnerware and food items and bring them forward so that her camp was at least set up when they reached it.

One of those particularly long days, Mrs. Linde got in the wagon with me, so she arrived in camp with us and was able to start dinner and have camp ready to receive their wagon an hour or so later. She was a quiet woman who spoke when she felt she had something of import to say, which was a lot more often when Mr. Linde was not around. Not only that, I noticed she wore a smile a lot more, especially those evenings when Brad delivered her to camp before her husband arrived.

The slope of the mountain continued to get steeper over these past few days. And now we were preparing for Jenny Creek Slide, as it was called. There would be considerable clearing to do. The oxen would be unhooked as the wagons were lowered down the hill. I didn't expect any arguments this time, however. Folks knew what could happen when an over-loaded wagon got loose on a steep hill.

We were going through the camp tonight and checking on wagons, stock, and everyone's frame of mind. The folks on the trail had really come together to help each other over these days and nights on the trail. I guessed it was because we were all sharing the same dreams.

The Lindes were actually feeling pretty good about tomorrow. It had been a long spell since they were not to come in last.

Chapter Fourteen

TENSION WAS THICKER THAN a slab of molasses bacon as wagons were lowered by ropes down the Jenny Creek Slide. Faces were etched with worry and tension.

I have to believe this is going to be all right.

Everyone had become so close during this trip that no one wanted to see anyone hurt or possessions lost and strung out all over the hillside. Especially since we had made it this far.

All 19 wagons started to line up. One team at a time was unhitched, and the oxen were moved aside and down the hillside, away from the path of the descending wagons. All the family members who were not holding a rope or guiding a wagon were also taken to the bottom of the hill. They waited there until all the wagons were safely moved down the steep decline.

Trees dotted the landscape, not leaving a clear path for the wagon, but with the right maneuvering, it was certainly manageable. Once again, everyone listened; no one got in front of the wagon. The owners got behind it so they could manage the tongue and guide it as best as possible, keep it from getting hung up by guiding it around the occasional tree, just a smidge here and there.

When the wagon reached bottom, each owner, with heavy leather gloves on, guided it completely out of the path of the next wagon by re-hitching the oxen, and then pulling it away from the path. Then he returned up the incline to take his spot on the rope, making sure nothing trailed him that would tangle, and allowing the next owner to take his position at the back of his own wagon. Out here on the trail, it was important that each traveler took responsibility for their own rig and its safety, and not expect someone else to do it for you.

There was only one exception. One of the older travelers, Shorty, refused to get down from his wagon. "I made the whole trip thus far," he said, "and I'm not much good at walking, so I'll see it to the bottom, one way or t'other." Brad agreed to let him do it because of his inability to walk on his own. Shorty hung on and leaned his aged body to move with the wagon. He was small and wiry. He never made a peep, even when the wagon came astride a rock for a short time. I knew I was not the only one holding my breath. But by golly, he rode it down, never complaining once.

When it came time for my wagon, Chase stepped up and said he would take my turn. I could, however, help by keeping the young'uns back and clear of any runaway wagons, which I had been doing anyway.

It was slow, hard labor that day, and labor it was. Without so much as a sneeze, everyone worked toward the common goal of going down that slide, one wagon, full of one lifetime, one roll of the wheels at a time, hand over hand, shoulder to shoulder, and grunt by grunt. You could hear the dried grass move under the wheels of the wagon along with the warning sound of a rock hiding in a clump of grass. Warning sounds that we learned to appreciate early on.

Nineteen wagons reached the bottom safely that day. What a happy bunch we were that night. It wouldn't be our last trip down a mountainside in that fashion, but for at least that moment, all had arrived safely. We were learning to count our blessings one hour at a time.

We settled for the night, as best we could, in a small clearing not so far from the bottom of the hill.

The oxen were content and rested, although I knew that they felt the stress of the day and the ordeal that some of us had experienced for the first, but certainly not the last, time.

That night, the campfires were small and few. We had access to lots of rocks, so we made high walls around our fire pit. The pit was mostly to warm the beans and more importantly to cook a pot of hickory coffee, the liquid that fueled us all. It kept us moving and aware.

Hickory coffee was made from hickory nuts that had been cracked and basically "shucked" before putting them in the pot to boil. It was a very rich, nutty, oily, and tasty concoction. My traveling companions drank it strong, scalding hot, and "barefooted," meaning black. If it wasn't strong, it was considered "dehorned bellywash" or "brown gargle." I figured if I were sharing coffee that I made, I'd better get it right the first time. No one wanted to be guilty of serving "bellywash."

Before traveling west, I had heard that a cowboy would sometimes be in the saddle for more than 24 hours, and his black coffee was what held him upright and awake so he could continue watch over his herd.

I drank more tea back home, but tea was still considered somewhat of a British habit, so unless you were female and serving it at some genteel gathering, coffee it was, for everyone, me included, at every meal. When it was convenient, and I was alone, I tended to add a touch of molasses to my coffee for a more soothing drink.

Tonight was a good time to catch up with Mary Parker. She was so torn from just birthing two children and only having one live. I didn't know what to say to her or how to console, so I didn't say much, but to admire her little Nikolas. He was more of a charmer by the hour. The other children adored him and did their best to be aware that their Ma needed a little more of their attention as well.

I didn't mean to say that we were not paying attention to Ned Parker. Surely we were, but just more discreetly. Ned and Mary were fully aware of their loss of little Margaret, but also so thankful for all of their living children. They would, I hoped, thrive once we were all settled.

I spoke briefly with Adam tonight. He was such a nice young man. I noticed that in the short time that I'd known him, he had matured. How could he not, with driving a team, taking on the caring of his siblings, as well as his family team of oxen, and, on many days, my team of oxen. He also had an enigmatic smile ever since he met Emily. I imagined that we would see a lot more of that with both Adam and Emily. *Oh to be young again, or at least as young as he and Emily are.*

We were in Oregon Territory, and that brought a certain feeling to me, and to others, of satisfaction that we would make it to "Eden," that place in the Oregon land where the streams and rivers reflected our images, fish jumped six feet, the deer were fat, there was lots of lush fertile land for growing healthy crops, and plenty of trees for building a new home.

Brad and Chase both joined me tonight as I ate my dried biscuit and small serving of beans and backstrap, companioned by my hickory coffee with molasses. I questioned them thoroughly about Oregon and if I had pictured it well from Nolan's second-hand description. "That's not so far from the truth," Brad said. "It is a rich land. But it is rich and unspoiled, because it's not an easy land to reach or conquer."

Brad had traveled on a previous wagon train a few years earlier that was going further north in the Oregon Territory. He reiterated that it had its own perils. He said, "If a man, or a woman, could hang on and get there intact, it was worth it. A lovelier place I've never seen."

"Is there anything more that I could do to assure that I'll make it?" I asked Brad.

"It would be wise to check your food stores and whenever we are in an area that has berries, wild onions, hickory, any type of food that can be brought into the wagon," he said, "you should gather it and store it. Also, when we're in an area where we can have a fire at night, it would be wise to fix a little extra food to eat as we travel, and to eat at night where no campfire will be allowed. Getting hungry doesn't work well when trying to get along with others."

He also finished that by saying, "You've done well at following instructions and being helpful. Keep doing that, and pray."

Chapter Fifteen

The next morning, everyone was ready to roll early. We were in a small clearing, but there was still quite a lot of vegetation. Brad had told us he wanted us to grab something to eat on the way. He was not a fan of campers being spread out or of trees or terrain blocking the wagons from each other. Campfires were tough to have as well. Brad sent Dennis ahead to scout for tonight's camp and to check out the terrain.

Adam was helping with my team—him leading and me driving from the wagon seat—with two of his siblings in the wagon. His older sister was driving her wagon as her Pa, Mr. Parker, led their team and kept a close watch on Mary, the new little Parker, and the remainder of his family.

As I watched Adam throughout the day, his smile was brighter than before. He'd always been a good-natured young man and helpful in all ways, but today he seemed to have a special sparkle in his eyes. I was pretty sure I knew the reason.

Around noon, we started to see a nice open area, although it did have some large boulders that required close attention. No quicker way to bust a wagon wheel than to hit a big rock. They didn't bend much.

Brad told us to stop for a brief rest and allow everyone to catch up. We took water and food, paid close attention to our animals, and took some personal privy time in the trees with a companion close by. We were there for a couple of hours. It gave those of us up front some time to chat a little while those toward the back of the train caught up and had some time of their own.

Adam asked his Pa if he could walk back in the lineup of wagons for a little to see how everyone was doing. His Pa was unaware that Adam was wearing an extra-special look today. His Pa, Ned, was too busy thinking about the new wee one and the rest of his family. Adam had permission, but only to be gone briefly in order to be ready to roll again on Brad's orders. The young man actually was whistling as he walked away, promising not to be gone long.

I checked on Mary Parker and the new addition. Then I took the kettle and put beans in it with some backstrap that Mary had, added enough water to cover the dry beans, put the lid on it, and put it in the back of my wagon. Hopefully the water wouldn't get sloshed out along the way. I hung the pot from a board that I put across the sides of the wagon about midway the length, so there would not be as much motion. Being careful not to put it over anything I wanted to keep dry, just in case.

There was also some wild sage that I collected while we were stopped. I gathered that, along with a small pot of blackberries, with the assistance of Jeremiah Parker and his big sister. They would taste great around tonight's camp meal.

We headed out that afternoon, not knowing where we would camp that night, but feeling refreshed and confident that whatever presented itself, we, as a group, could handle it.

Dennis met us late afternoon and said we should stop within two hours. There was a great place up ahead near a small creek winding down the hill into a beautiful valley. We would camp near the creek tonight, and all would be within sight of each other. There would be circling of the first five wagons and the last four, but the ones in the middle would be in a straight line. It was just the way the terrain was laid out. We were excited, however, because this gave folks an opportunity to get a little better acquainted with their traveling companions, and group meals were always more congenial. I was sure glad I had put that pot of beans on to soak. I checked them to make sure they still had water and added another cup or so of creek water.

Around five that afternoon, we started to circle the first five wagons, unhitching our teams and gathering them close in, but leaving adequate room for our firepits and, of course, enough room to gather and meet with our traveling neighbors. I got that pot of beans on a fire even before unhitching and taking care of my team. Even now, they still wouldn't be thoroughly cooked for a couple of hours.

It was some time before everyone was stopped for the night and settled in. But we had a dandy spot right along Bear Creek. Not sure why they called it that, but based on my earlier bear experience, I intend to keep open ears and eyes and to have some protection nearby.

After water was gathered and the animals were all watered and taken care of, there was another opportunity for a bath. Only this time, we had the husbands guarding with guns as their wives and children bathed. Even though their backs were turned to those of us that were in the water, they stayed close by with guns at the ready. Chase and Brad were up and down the riverbank at all times, making sure that everyone was at the ready.

By the time all of this was done, dinner smelled pretty good. Keeping in mind, that if we could smell those vittles, the animals could smell them even better. Anything that had a scent and wasn't being cooked was high up in a tree and wrapped tight or in a tight container. We didn't want any bear visiting the camp and especially not climbing into a wagon with us.

I made a point of inviting Chase and Brad for dinner tonight to our cookfire. They both came around, each carrying a little something to add to the evening's meal. Chase brought molasses for the biscuits that someone else had cooked. Brad brought a nice can of huckleberries that he had picked along the trail today. They were a real treat and scarce in many locales.

Everyone pitched in for cleanup after dinner. All food scraps were wrapped for the road tomorrow and stored in tight containers so as not to attract the animals. It was amazing how it only took one or two incidents to make a real impression, especially when you felt like you might be the entree.

After supper, Chase quietly took my hands in his.

"Will you take a short walk with me?" he asked.

"I'd be pleased," I said.

He tucked my hand on his arm as he carried his rifle in his other hand. He also had a large Bowie knife on his waist belt. The Bowie knife was invented in 1838 for close contact fighting. I was pretty sure he wouldn't have been carrying it if he didn't know how to use it.

He made me feel so safe, and yet he made my stomach tumble at the same time. When he smiled at me, or inclined his head with the slightest tip of his hat, I just got all twisted up. I started smiling like a fool. I hadn't caught myself drooling yet, but there was always tomorrow. We walked along quiet at first, then he pulled my arm a little tighter to his side as he studied me from the side. Pretty soon he stopped and looked into my eyes, and then he said, "I don't want to give you a lick of trouble or have folks talkin' and guessing about us, especially about you. But Questa, you're so darn pretty that sometimes I can't express myself very well to you. But more than that, I just can't get enough of you. You know, your talking, the sound of your voice, the way you pitch in along the trail, and just your grit. You're the dangdest woman I ever met, especially to be so young. I hope you don't mind that I said that to you, but darn it, I sure meant every word."

Looking right back at him, I countered, "Chase, thank you for such kind things that you're saying about me. I'm just trying to carry my weight and am nothing special. Besides, I'm not that young, and I do like it that you enjoy my company, because I enjoy yours, too."

He smiled. "Your age is just right, and I intend to get to know you even better, day by day."

"Those are my very wishes as well," I said.

We continued on down the line of wagons but separated ourselves a little more, so I wasn't right up against him for the sheer pleasure of his hard body. This way I still could balance on his arm, but not look too forward to others and start their tongues a-wagging.

On the way back to the wagon, we ran into Adam Parker. He said he was checking in on the rest of the folks, making sure they were all settled for the night. This was the second time today that he "was checking on the folks in the back." The lilt in his walk and his determined path gave Chase and I both reason to believe that he had a clear destination in mind. I did notice that the young man was now carrying his own rifle. I could see that he had been reminded by his father or by Brad that there must be a good reason for the creek being called Bear Creek. It was best to be prepared for whatever came his way.

Here was what I learned. Those bears, most of the time, were not stopped by one shot, unless it hit the perfect mark. And you had to have the time to aim the rifle. A charging bear wasted no time wondering if you were going to hit him or not. He just kept on coming until his brain told his body it was over, and he caused a lot of damage in the process. That was another good reason to wear a Bowie knife, as well as carrying a gun. Of course, it helped if you knew how to shoot and were precise, in addition to being able and willing to wield a knife against man or beast.

Chapter Sixteen

THE NIGHT PASSED QUIETLY without any disturbances or any uninvited four-legged animals in camp. Brad had someone on duty all night. A man was posted with a rifle at the ready at the end of the train on each side of the wagons. They walked, for their shift, from one end to the other, sweeping the trail as they went and keeping each other in sight. Each shift was two hours. They started at dusk and lasted until daybreak.

We'd been lucky so far on this trip. Most of us still had decent food supplies, especially with us sharing amongst ourselves in community pots and picking wild berries and herbs along the way during the past couple of weeks.

However, a few were getting lower on things like flour, a food staple for someone crossing the miles. Of course, we didn't have eggs, even though a couple of the wagons had a few chickens with them. Eggs were scarcer than hen's teeth, and you know how scarce those were!

The men, and the women, were keeping wild animals in mind, not only because they could hurt us physically, but because they offered us a great source of food protein that would keep us healthier than any flour could. We also had to be especially mindful of what traps we set for fish or rabbit, for fear of providing an open invitation to a bear.

Blackberry bushes were prolific. But as tasty as they were, those bushes were terrible hard to get through if you were trying to pass through in a wagon, or on foot, for that matter. The vines were tough and grew forever, and the thorns, being strong and sharp, penetrated our clothing.

Tonight, we were thankful after making it through yet another day bringing us continued anticipation of what yet awaited us. We were celebrating with fresh-picked blackberries made into several savory cobblers that we shared. A couple of harmonicas tuned up and played a few easy tunes before we turned in.

In between shifts tonight, several of the men took the time to clean their rifles and reload ammo to be at the ready, still being mindful of guarding the weary travelers. I put another pot of beans in to soak for dinner for the Parkers and me tomorrow night. Mary Parker was still keeping pretty quiet and to herself, but it was always a pleasure to talk with her. She was loving towards her husband and children.

There was such pain and quiet hurt behind her eyes. And yet she readied herself, little Nikolas, and the remaining family members each day with her positive attitude and sweet smile.

We had the lean-to fixed off the side of the wagon again, giving the children a dry, starless ceiling to sleep under and stay close to their parents. They were so tired at night that the whispers barely lasted five minutes before quiet seeped into the surrounding night.

For those dreaming of traveling and setting up a life in the West, it was not easy. The trip itself took planning. Most of the families that traveled together had 10 family members, sometimes more, sometimes less. Carrying enough food and clothing for that many was alone a hardship.

The wagons were usually 36 to 48 inches wide on the inside, and up to eight or nine feet long. Most travelers had a pair of oxen with a third trailing behind the wagon to be rotated, and a smaller, 36-inch-wide wagon. We did have one Conestoga that was 48 inches wide and 12 feet long, carrying a family of 10 with another on the way. They used a six-up hitch of oxen.

Most wagons started with 1,000 pounds of food. Flour, sugar, salt, dried meat, coffee, rice, beans, and hardtack were typical. The Robertson family started with 1,500 pounds and would run out at some point if they didn't harvest along the way.

That meant that families walked across the prairie; they didn't ride, in order to accommodate their food and personal items. Because I was a single wagon owner, I was one of the lucky ones who was able to ride.

I didn't leave with this group when Nalan and I left Fort Hall. We were playing catch-up the whole time, until he got sick and died, of course. Then it was me following what little trail I could find and hoping for the best. It didn't make sense to go back, so I pushed forward. And mighty glad that I did.

Our water barrels had been refilled with water last night. It revealed to several of us that the paraffin needed to be re-set in some of our barrels. We couldn't do it tonight in the dark, but we would do it first light tomorrow morning before leaving camp. We couldn't chance the barrels starting to leak and lose water while we were out on the trail.

Chapter Seventeen

For the next five days, we kept to our order in the train, except for the Robertson wagon: a Conestoga with six oxen pulling for a family of 10. It was a heavy wagon, even before the food was loaded. It was waterproofed with tar, known to be heavy but durable, so that it could keep water out when crossing the many rivers in our future.

Brad wanted the Robertson family closer to the front of the line where he could keep an eye on everything, including the amount of help that was available from the Parkers, and from Chase and from me. They were moved into the fourth position, Chase into the third position, and Brad moved me into the fifth position.

I took two of the younger Robertson children into my wagon to ride. This was a huge help, since the Robertson family already had a heavy load and young children who could not walk that fast. Sarah, age five, and James, age six, were as sweet as the Parker children, and no problem for me at all, except sometimes I had to shush them because of their sheer volume. Even more important, Brad thought it safer to have the small children hidden from the view of the big cat that we'd seen more signs of recently. It appeared that he was tracking us.

The wagon wheels creaked as we made our way through bushes and some blackberry vines. We were fortunate that in some areas, prior wagons had already rolled through, and the trail had been cleared. Not all areas, however. In some areas, it was almost as if the blackberry vines took a deep breath and shot out more, thicker vines. They were certainly a deterrent to easy travel.

Adam was in heaven. Emily was one of the Robertson family. With them moved up in line formation, it made it easier for him to "check on those in back," which was what we heard a lot of prior to reforming the order of the wagons.

In addition, Mrs. Robertson was in a family way, and Brad was trying to reassure her that there would be help as her time advanced. I wondered what would happen when the Parker girl met the Robertson boy, Will. Would be very interesting to see if more romantic interests or liaisons formed on this journey.

The Robertson family started with a bigger wagon to haul more food, but the size of their family had sorely depleted their resources. Flour was all but gone, sugar was low, and beans were getting scarcer by the day for them. I had more food than anyone, since my wagon was loaded for two. With Nalan gone, there was just me. So each day I took it upon myself to cook a larger pot of beans and fix more biscuits. I never did learn to just cook for one.

Besides, I invited Chase—who had his own food supplies—and Brad to join me most nights, so extra was always needed. I asked the Robertson children if they could furnish berries and wild-grown onions as they became available. It was definitely a community effort. It was everyone's responsibility to take turns feeding Brad, the wagon master. He did not have a wagon to carry supplies for himself, so we saw him many nights for dinner. Chase had his own supplies, but stayed busy helping everyone with their wagons. It made good sense to include him in our meals. He was delighted to share food and have me cook it.

I liked Emily and totally understood Adam's fascination with the young woman. She was quiet, helpful, funny, and loved her family. But her smile was what won over Adam; it made the sun shine when she shared it. She had walked next to my wagon much of the time in case she needed to help with her siblings in the wagon. She had a sister, Betha, who was one year older, who was watching over her mother and the other younger children around their wagon, although they were older and didn't have problems keeping up. Besides, Emily was closer to Adam now as well.

Though it had taken several days and reminders, I learned the rest of the family names. The parents were Anna and Joseph. Son Jesse was 18, Will was 15, Jacob was 10, and Clara was 12.

They didn't have much of anything else in the wagon but food provisions. That was what they started with, which meant their personal items were pretty much forfeited at the beginning of the trip, except for bedding and bathing needs.

They were uncomplaining. They were excited about the prospects of their new opportunities out West.

I saw Emily step to the side of the trail today. She had an eye for wild spices, root plants, and berries. She kept our taste buds awake with her finds. It sounded odd, but she also acted as a barometer on what animals were close by. Of course they left droppings, so her awareness gave us a time and a type of animal to be on the ready for. She could also distinguish by their tracks if they were moving quickly or grazing.

Brad asked Will and Jacob to keep an eye on everyone's water barrels since we did not re-paraffin them yet. The water level needed to be down because of water usage, not losing it due to leaks, before they could re-paraffin the inside of our barrels.

Will and Jacob were also sharing duty with their father by walking alongside the oxen to make sure they were not being lazy and were keeping to the trail. Their mother, Anna, traded off riding and walking to keep from getting stiff, but also to assure herself that she was staying physically able when it came time to birth. The docs, many times, told expectant mothers that exercise in moderation, especially walking, was a good practice for ease of delivery. At least that was what my Ma repeated to me.

Tonight when we stopped, Jacob Robertson, the 10-year-old, was hurting something awful. Seems he got some type of burr in his shoe, as well as rubbing a painful blister on the bottom of his foot, which that burr found a home in. The bottom of his shoe was worn clean through, so there was no protection left where he blistered.

I, along with his Ma, prepared a tub of clean water to clean his foot and pull the burr off as best we could, trying to locate all the small pieces of it. At that point, I placed a piece of fat bacon around his foot and wound it with a strip of clean cloth before putting one of my clean socks over it to hold it in place. He had orders to ride in the wagon with his Ma tomorrow and possibly the next day until his foot healed.

I was glad I had some bacon readily available. It was best for removing any poison that could be in a sore and for removing those small pieces of burr we could not see with our eyes. Dennis asked for his shoe that night in camp. He used a piece of a pelt that he had cured, to fix the hole in the shoe.

We didn't always have the luxury of being able to clean a wound, doctor it, and stay off it, but when we did, we took advantage of it. More than anything, he needed a little personal care from his Ma. The trip was hard on all ages.

One of the wagons toward the back of the train got a surprise last night. Large cat prints were spotted around their wagon, although the cat did not attack or attempt to enter their camp. They were fortunate. We were all alerted and on the ready. *You can be sure tonight we will be even more vigilant, knowing that the cat is tracking us.*

There was some discussion about Indians last night, since we were in the Rogue Indian territory. So far there had been no sign of them and no word of any trouble. The stories that we heard before leaving the fort supposedly came from the Applegate brothers on their initial expedition of the Applegate Trail. They mentioned more than once that the Indians could be a problem on other parts of the trail, but not so much on the southern route of the Oregon Trail. Other pioneers would later refer to that route as the Applegate Trail in honor of the brothers who founded it.

We were mentally trying to prepare ourselves for this next part of our journey, checking the yokes on the oxen and the hitches on the horses. The land was changing again. It was heavily wooded, even with travelers clearing the trail just months before us. There was steep terrain and more rocks lurking in the tall bush and grass to damage our wagon wheels. We were told to get wagon wheel maintenance materials readily available in case we had broken wheels, which would be almost impossible to avoid. We didn't want to be digging for supplies when it happened.

As we got to higher elevation, we also had to be aware of more wild animals and the poisonous timber rattlers. The weather was cooling a little with fall close at hand, but they were still able to strike without much warning. We needed to be aware because we were not familiar with their warning sounds, which were much different than that of a desert rattlesnake.

We were warned to check out our surroundings and watch where we stepped. We couldn't afford to have an ox bitten, and we certainly didn't want our travelers bitten. We did have some ammonia with us to put on bites, but typically we would cut out the snakebite portion to try to get ahead of the venom. Cutting skin meant a larger possibility of an infection, or losing a limb, or losing feeling in the affected area, or worse.

When Brad called the wagon meeting tonight, he asked us to check our wagons and our stock before attending. He proceeded during the meeting to ask each one of us with an extra pair of oxen to hook them up tomorrow.

"For those towing one extra oxen or horse," he said, "interchange it with one of our weaker animals or put one of the children or another family member on it. Take the load off as best we can while traversing this next incline."

Jacob, by this time, had developed a headache and a throbbing foot. He was told by Mrs. Brahm to ride in the back of his wagon tomorrow with his foot elevated.

Chapter Eighteen

As near as Brad and I could figure, we had 100 or so folks on this journey. That number would continue to change as babies were birthed along the way and, sadly, as others would perish.

First thing this morning, Misters Linde and Ross approached the front of the train and wanted to speak to Brad about their circumstances.

It seemed that they and their wives had talked quite extensively about how they could help each other out. Since the Lindes had been placed to the back of the train with only one ox, making their wagon slower, even after unloading many personal possessions, and the Rosses were in back with two oxen and no wagon, after it splintered on the hillside along with their personal home goods, they had formed an alliance.

Both wanted the ability to move up, at times, to other locations in the train so as not to be exhausted by evening when they arrived in camp. They had come up with a solution that sounds doable.

The Rosses had two oxen left, but no wagon. The Lindes had a wagon (lightened), with only one ox due to losing the other in the river. They had discussed hooking the two oxen, belonging to the Rosses, to the wagon owned by the Lindes. They would have a spare ox behind the wagon that could carry the few articles of the Rosses that were not destroyed, if it were necessary.

Brad agreed that this sounded like a good idea as long as they could all get along. Based on their past, this was not an unrealistic question to ask them. The menfolk commented that they'd been traveling next to each other for several days and were OK. It also gave the womenfolk some company, being able to talk to each other and set up camp at night. In addition, they could add a tarp to the side of the wagon at night so that the Rosses would have some nighttime protection against frost or rain.

Brad asked Mr. Gil to lead off and keep a slow pace with Dennis showing us the way, while he also was being diligent about scouting for unwelcome visitors. Brad was moving to the back to assist the Ross and Linde families with the transferring and the switching of their oxen and belongings. He also wanted to check out the others toward the back of the train. A couple of families toward the back had a passel of kids.

Mrs. Robertson and I checked Jacob this morning before rolling a wheel. He still has a throbbing foot and a bad headache. The foot felt better when elevated. Mrs. Robertson fixed him a cup of ginger tea this morning, and I had a peppermint stick for him to wallow around his mouth. Between the tea and the peppermint, he should have gotten rid of his headache and calmed his stomach. Hopefully, posthaste.

As Brad and the misters moved toward the back, they carried on an easy conversation. "How is Rush Spencer integrating with you?" he asked. "And is everyone getting along?"

Interestingly enough, Brad heard that Rush had put some modest moves on Betha Robertson, age 17, before they moved forward in the lineup, and very quickly, 18-year-old Titus Ross shut him down without a punch being thrown.

As I mentioned before, Rush Spencer was not a small man by any means. However, Titus was a strapping young man who was raised on a farm and worked in a blacksmith shop. His chest and arms were as large as my upper legs and solid as any piece of iron I'd ever seen. He was a quiet young man, not boastful, but he made sure that Rush Spencer knew that he would use his young, brute force to make a point if Rush ever attempted to molest any woman on the train again. He was especially vehement and showed it when he puffed up bigger and prettier than any peacock I ever did see. He made his point.

Between the deterrent of Titus, Chase, and Brad, Rush Spencer had about run clean out of luck. He'd made enemies at both ends of the wagon line now. As Brad shared this with Chase and me, I couldn't help thinking that if I were Rush, I'd be stepping real lightly. I swore he was a dead man wasting air with his behavior.

Titus certainly got Betha's attention. Not only was she thankful for his intervention, but she was not as timid as I had once thought. She placed a hand on his forearm and asked him if he could join them in her camp tomorrow night to meet her family. She thanked him once again while holding her blue eyes steady on his.

Brad assisted the misters in switching the yokes and harnesses on the two oxen as they hitched them to the wagon. Mrs. Linde took the one extra ox and tied him to the back of the now-shared wagon. Misses Linde and Ross put what items the Rosses were currently carrying on their oxen into the wagon. Brad shared that it was amazing to watch the smiles break out on the ladies' faces as they considered that they would be able to keep up today, as well as have company as they moved forward.

Rush Spencer was not only the last in the line; he was the last on everyone's list, especially Brad's. Brad would do everything he could to let Rush know his behavior wouldn't be tolerated and was unwelcome.

He told Rush the truth, but he also put some worry into him. "We're being tracked by at least one big cat and maybe more," Brad told Rush. "You need to be carrying your loaded gun at all times and be on the lookout. Cats are likely to stalk the weakest part of the train. In this case, it's the last wagon in line. Your time should be spent on your animals, your wagon, and that cat. Not on the women on the train."

Brad also told Rush to, "Give me a holler, if you can, should that cat come a-callin." Rush was a bit nervous after their little tête-à-tête. Understandably though, he was very aware of what was going on around him.

The train had rolled forward and soon the Ross and the Linde families made up the short distance to the other wagons from their lapsed start. Their wagon and their oxen seemed to be working well.

Mrs. Ross drove from the seat while Mrs. Linde walked beside the head of the right ox. Misters Linde and Ross walked on either side of the back of the wagon and spare ox, with loaded guns and watchful eyes. At lunchtime, the women would switch the driver and walking positions, keeping it fair. Of course, Rush Spencer was behind them, taking up the very rear as the last wagon. Brad's efforts were working. Spencer was so busy trying to keep an eye on everything, he had no time to even say hello.

Two wagons in front of the Linde and Ross families was the Whittacker family, husband and wife, somewhere between young and middle in age, hardworking, and always willing to pitch right in.

They had an arrangement with Rocky, one of the outriders that was on the trip. He was a good trail scout and horse handler. Also was a mite alright when he aimed and shot at a target. Since he was on horseback, he needed some place to carry his food supplies. The Whittacker family agreed to carry them. Mrs. Whittacker fixed his meals as well. In exchange, Rocky helped to take care of their oxen, worked on the wagon any way that was needed, and also took care of other camp duties. He was a great hand with the rest of the wagons as well, and, did I mention, he was a great scout. Between him and Dennis, they had the scouting well handled.

He and Mr. Whittacker worked well together, both showing respect for the other. That alone was worth more than 10 bags of flour. This trip could really get to you. The tension, the fear of the unknown, no privacy, leaving family and possessions behind, and running out of food, just to name a few. You were miles ahead and had already won if you got along with your traveling companions.

The Braham family was somewhere midway in the train lineup. They started this trip with seven children and early on lost two along the way. How sad that must have been. To start this trip with so many dreams for your family, only to lose them. One boy was run over by a wagon when the boy was playing under it as the train readied to move. His brother got bit by something out on the trail and swelled up before anything could be done. His was a terrible death.

Their Mama felt at fault and was ashamed, blaming herself for not keeping a better eye on them. Her husband, sad and distraught though he was, told her that she couldn't be everywhere at once. She told Mr. Brahm that if that were the case, they shouldn't have more children and would be taking extra precautions about getting with child again. I actually think that was probably a good idea until they were settled and had a home. Although, each morning I prayed that nothing happened to the remaining children of any of the families.

I found myself becoming more and more aware of what was around me. How it felt, how it smelled, and how it sounded. For instance, it made a difference what you heard if you were walking or riding on the wagon. So many sounds were masked if you were riding. Like the groaning and creaking of the wood as it gives, or the wagon wheels, rimmed in a metal ring around the wood circle and spokes, running over the rocks or the tall bushes as they whooshed through the hills and the valleys layered with greenery and dried bushes of every color and texture. Some places were like looking at a quilt, or maybe a tapestry was a better word.

When you walked, the sounds were more personal, and close up to you, with your ears being super sensitive and sounds seeming almost touchable.

Speaking of sounds, Mr. Wiggins, the owner of the wagon directly in front of the Brahm family, had two children, nearing grown, at least the boy Tanner was, at 16. I heard from others rolling toward the back of the wagon line that those two children talked a lot. They had some great conversations, of which the Brahm family didn't hear much until the train stopped for the night. Tanner and his 14-year-old sister, Kate, challenged each other and didn't care who heard it. Mr. Wiggins appeared to be not only used to their chatter, but expected and probably enjoyed it. They were not rude or loud, but nonstop.

They were both good children and sounded very educated. I understood from speaking with Brad that Kate wanted to be a schoolteacher. She was witty and quick to find intelligent answers.

They were very helpful to their father and to each other. Tanner was up and usually hooking up the oxen in the mornings before his father did, and Kate was very adept around a cookfire and at keeping laundry caught up when washing facilities could be found. Mr. Wiggins, a widower, was a pleasant-acting and looking man. His wife died in childbirth about five years prior. Since then, he had raised his two children with the guidance of his mother who had also since succumbed. At that point, he decided to move west and start anew.

Today as we traveled, we noticed more signs of prior travelers that had come the same path that we had chosen, or at least crossed our trail at some point.

We also saw a sign of a cat. Paw prints were seen at one higher elevation that we crossed. It was as if he were watching us as he circled, first in front and then behind. According to Dennis, our tracker, the cat print was large and thought to be a mountain lion, also known as a cougar. There were many in these parts of the territory. He said it was a very large cat. Even with his claws retracted, the print was much larger than a man's open hand. Cougars liked to feed on deer, but we'd seen more cat prints the last couple of weeks than we'd seen of deer. The large feline appeared to be considering a change in his diet.

Around noon, we stopped the wagons to take some relief. We were not allowing folks to wander off for privacy with the cat so close. We were trying to get as many of the children and women in the wagons as possible to make them less of a target. Of those women, Mrs. Linde was now on the seat with Mrs. Ross.

Ross' nephew, Titus, was now roaming with his loaded gun between the end of the train up to about four wagon-lengths. He offered protection for stock and children while parents were relieving themselves and managing their wagon setup.

Just as everyone had readjusted their riding positions, we heard a mountain lion scream. It was our "ghost cat," our stalker. It was loud and scared me to the bone. He was close by now, letting us know that he was coming for us. But when? *Do we sit here and wait? Or keep moving?*

"Move!" Brad ordered. "Now!"

Children, not yet in their teens, needed to be in a wagon or walking as far from the bushes as possible. Parents quickly made arrangements, deciding what their oxen could pull and who could keep up while walking.

"Everyone else who knows how to shoot and is accurate, ready your arms," Brad said. "If you have a knife, have it handy in case your shot misses the mark. We are to keep moving until we find a wide-open space to camp close together and, wherever possible, away from the brush."

Mountain lions were known as cougars, but many times referred to as "ghost cats." The latter because they were a tawny color and blended quickly and easily into the brush and trees, which acted like a natural camouflage. By the time they have shown themselves, it was too late for their victims. Hence, we knew to stay away from the brush.

We heard the cat a couple more times in the next three hours of travel. Stopping at a good-sized clearing, we were told to circle the wagons and bring the stock inside that circle, so they wouldn't be as easily attacked. We were told to take our metal firepits, if we had them, and place them outside the circled wagons and put a fire in them—not to cook, but rather to discourage cats or bears from attacking. We built some solid fires in the inner circle with lots of rock surrounding them for our safety. We cooked communally that night, everyone sharing, guards taking turns around the circle, being careful not to look directly at the fires, so as not to blind ourselves, even though temporarily.

In the grey light of day, the screaming of the cat pierced the early morning quiet. As many were getting their eyes open, our guards came to full attention as the scream shredded the air. Two shots were fired just outside of the Brahms wagon. At once, the children inside the wagon started to roust. All but one stayed out of sight.

The youngest was trying to get out to relieve himself. Evidently the cat saw him at the same time that Titus saw the cat. His first shot hit the cat in the rib cage as the cat was about to leap. Mr. Brahm got off the second shot in the animal's neck from the opposite side. The cat was down. Mr. Brahm warily approached the cat, his eyes still open, teeth bared slightly. The cat twitched; Mr. Brahm put a final bullet into the cat's head.

An audible sigh came from the circled encampment, inside and outside of the wagons. Those who had stood guard all night let their shoulders relax and gathered their families.

The first duty of the day was to skin and prepare the meat of the cat for future meals to share tonight. Dennis, Rocky, and Ben, our other single outrider, took care of the meat and carcass so we could continue getting ready for whatever the day would bring us.

"Even though you don't have to be as super vigilant you've been," Brad told all of us, "we should not let our guards down in case there's more than one animal around."

With the cat dead, due to Titus's quick first shot, and because of Mr. Brahm getting the kill-shot in, tonight we would eat well again, and Titus met and supped with Betha's family.

Chapter Nineteen

Titus was pretty much on top of his morning, and it carried him throughout the day. Now it wouldn't be right to think that he took the shooting of the cat lightly, because he sure didn't. But truth to tell, he was smiling so big because he was going to see Betha tonight, and supp with her family at her direct invitation. He wasn't exactly whistling, but rather, kind of blowing through his teeth. Some might even have said he had a ridiculous look on his face. I didn't see him until that evening when he showed up at the Robertson camp. At that point, I read his face as a young man, totally smitten, and from looking at Betha, I think the feeling was mutual.

Supper was a pretty special affair, even though the food was simple and sparse. By this time on the trail, our food was quite limited. We had some dried squash and apples and a small amount of beans stored in the first couple of wagons. In addition to those food choices, I still had flour, salt, and bacon. Otherwise, we were becoming more dependent on the game killed along the way. Thankfully, in this highly wooded, brushy area, wild onions, berries, and mushrooms were quite prolific.

Titus had shone up shortly after getting his folks settled and their oxen taken care of for the night. He figured he had to make a good impression on Betha and her folks, so he took a few extra minutes to wash his face and neck with his wet kerchief, comb his hair, and shake the dust off his shirt. Although he seemed a little nervous, he stepped right up for introductions to Betha's parents and siblings. Even though Titus had met some of her family members in the past, this was more formal and had an edge. He wanted to let her family know that he and Betha were interested in more than just a passing hello. He needed the family's approval.

Titus talked easily with Jozeph, Betha's father, and helped to get the oxen settled for the night as they became better acquainted. It was also a great time for Betha's older brother, Jesse, to get to know Titus. Of course, everyone thought he was a hero for making the killing shot of the big mountain lion.

Speaking of cat, that was the main course on everyone's supper fare tonight. The stewpots and skillets all the way down the length of the wagon train simmered the lean meat. Some had added squash and onions to it while others chose to have their dried vegetables fixed in a more traditional skillet mix, which is what Mrs. Robertson and Betha had done.

The meat was first dipped lightly in a flour mixture containing salt, pepper, and some sliced mushrooms. Squash, onions, and a few white peas, which seemed to grow well in the area, were added for texture and flavor.

Overall, it was a delightful meal. The first five wagons participated in the food shares and the cooking at the Robertson's. That meant that Titus wasn't just under the scrutiny of the Robertson bunch, but also that of the Gills, the Parkers, Brad, and me. That added up to a passel of names and faces.

At some point after cleanup, a couple of mouth harps and a fiddle came out of the wagons, along with a washboard. After a wonderful dinner, being surrounded by great friends, the music was magical. This was better than any dance ever was at home back east. Other travelers joined in for the music.

Mr. and Mrs. Gill, never slacking, were the first to take the dance floor, which was actually grassy-packed, hard ground. Closely following were Mr. and Mrs. Robertson, young Titus and a glowing Betha. Their first dance steps were somewhat hesitant, but they caught on very quickly.

Chase's hand was proffered straight away as he held me far enough to see his smile before he pulled me closer, for appropriate dances, of course. On the faster dances, he held me close enough that I would not stumble or fall. I was close enough to see that he shaved tonight before coming to dinner. He also had attempted to shake the day off his clothes and had added a clean kerchief around his neck. His hands were hard and calloused, but he held me gently and without any force. I tended to want him to hold me closer as each dance progressed.

The young Robertson children were dancing with each other and were darling. The youngest, five-year-old Sarah Robertson, was gathered up between her mother and father on one dance, and they all danced together. Sarah was thrilled to be getting so much attention from her parents. Life on the trail was not easy or romantic most of the time. These moments were precious and not to be taken for granted.

Little Sarah eventually asked Chase to dance with her, and he very gallantly took her hand and twirled her around, which was what she wanted. When her Mother, Anna, finally came to put her to bed, she was ready and offered no resistance.

While Chase was dancing with lovely little Sarah, Brad took the opportunity to ask me to dance. He was a good dancer, handsome, and light on his feet. However, he didn't make me short of breath like Chase did.

Adam Parker got his chance and was dancing with Emily Robertson. They had become quite comfortable with each other over the weeks since they first met. It had helped with their wagon placement being closer together.

Ned and Mary danced a slow dance before retiring with baby Nikolas. Trish held sweet Nikolas while her parents shared that moment. Mary was healing both physically and emotionally from the loss of little Margaret. But the question always arose in my head, *"How does one get over losing a baby?" I will be her friend, and here if she needs me.*

Trish, at age 15, was kind of shy tonight, but 16-year-old Will Parker was not ignoring her, for sure. They had talked briefly around the dinners in the past few weeks, but tonight they were actually spending some uninterrupted time discussing topics and staring into the fire when they ran out of subject matter. They didn't quite yet appear to be ready for anything other than a friendship, which made sense, given their youth.

Back to Titus and Betha—one of the reasons for the group gathering tonight and the festiveness surrounding the supper. Titus had first asked Betha, which was a very smart move, if she would like to progress in their relationship. She resoundingly answered yes. Then he went to her parents and asked them for their permission. They had given their blessing with the understanding that he would honor her and not push for her favors before this trip was done, and that they had an opportunity to see each other in stable surroundings. Both had agreed. They held hands as they sauntered to a log and sat down.

The place that we chose as our camp tonight was an open area—heavily brushed some distance away, which gave us some feeling of comfort. Brad still asked for at least four volunteers throughout the night with loaded guns at the ready. He said that mountain lions usually had their own territories and didn't impinge on another cat's territory. Unless he or she were mating or parenting. To be safe, we had four volunteers for each three-hour shift, meaning eight volunteers. Brad also asked us to make our yard implements handy for tomorrow. According to Dennis, we had some clearing to do. He spread the word down the line as he got his volunteers for tomorrow.

We wouldn't be pulling out at our earliest in the morning. Betha, Emily, Trish, Kate, and I would be harvesting mushrooms, berries, onions, and any other wild herbs we could find, such as sage. We needed enough harvested food to keep us healthy. We had encouraged everyone to take some vinegar at least once a day. Its high Vitamin C content guarded against scurvy. Without fresh greens and fruit, we were very susceptible.

Brad mentioned this morning that Rush was starting to grumble again. Brad expected we'd be having more of his antics again before long. He said Rush was right about his position, that it was not fair that he always ended up in the back eating dust. Brad said that to be fair, he would be rearranging the wagons again soon. Although he hadn't told Rush that.

The night passed without any surprises. Breakfast was a small repast with food reserves becoming slim. I made a small amount of wheat cereal so the children could eat something that wasn't fussy, but would stick to their ribs. Hopefully, we would be able to glean a good amount of fresh food today.

After harvesting, we started on the trail about 10 a.m., which was late for us. We had been on the trail (more like traveling in the general direction of the trail) for about an hour when we approached an area so dense with vines that we could not get through. Dennis said this was what he meant when he told us we would have to chop our way through, because there was no way around it. We were at a standstill, but we had a hardy and helpful crew.

The scythe, a grass sickle, and a rake came forward with the hardy fellow travelers. Those implements, although wonderful in a grass field, would not budge the thick vines. Berry vines as much as a quarter-inch thick curved back and forth, over and under, and in-between. Again, we were at a standstill.

I did not know much about Mr. Whittacker. In fact, I still didn't. He turned and went back to his wagon after witnessing the thick overgrown and intimidating wall of thorns. A couple of the men who had tried to cut through the brush had been sliced by the thorns. Wounds were open and bleeding on many parts of their arms, legs, and chests. They were even cut on their faces. No one was running back into the brambles.

Everyone was deep in thought when Mr. Whittacker reappeared. That, in itself, would not have gotten my attention, but he returned with the biggest knife I'd ever seen.

There was room on the handle for two hands, men-size hands. The blade was thick and appeared to be heavy. The knife was very long, at least a foot and a half in length. He said it was called a machete and originated in Spain. It was also used by sailors to cut through ropes and to slice other "things that got in the way." I got the impression it was used in war. He asked us to step back as he stepped up to the vines and studied them.

His first slice through the air made contact with the fist of vines daring the men to approach. It sliced through them. He took another swing, this time lower to the ground. A section of the vines was now suspended without tension in it. Mr. Whittacker took a third slice through the air into the vines, then another below. He stepped back.

Titus, who had been very intent, stepped up and asked Mr. Whittacker if he could have a go at it. He had put on some very heavy gloves that he used when blacksmithing. Mr. Whittacker seemed glad for the reprieve. He showed Titus how to place his hands on the knife handle to get the best swing and connection. Titus handled the machete like it was natural for him. He sliced high, then low, just as Mr. Whittacker had demonstrated, only without stopping.

After about 20 minutes, Mr. Whittacker suggested those with grass hooks, scythes, and grass sickles bring them forward and use them to drag away the cut vines. They needed to be cleared away before we could cut deeper and eventually move through the wall of vines.

It was an hour or more when Titus, who was using the machete again, halted and looked quite quizzical. He stepped back, nodded to anyone still there, and asked, "What's that?"

Brad tried to get a better look, but was still uncertain. Mr. Whittacker took a look, turning his head to several different angles and finally said, "Looks like someone didn't make it, or at least their wagon didn't."

That got everyone fired up. They started taking turns at the machete. A wide swath had to be cleared, and it was some 20 feet thick. It was an impenetrable wall, at least until we took the machete to it.

By the time we could actually see the vine-infested buckboard clearly, we slowed our movements so as not to further damage the wagon. It appeared that the wagon had been left behind. Since there was a single hookup for only one ox, we figured it had died, leaving the travelers with no way to take the buckboard. The wagon was in pretty good shape. We just needed to cut vines from the spokes and the seat boards.

In the back of the wagon was a strong canvas bag that had an extra pair of rugged work pants and a jacket that would fit a large man, just about Titus' size. We made sure that Titus took them with him. There was also a metal bucket with a lid. Inside it we found hay and oats for the ox, along with a small can of liniment for man and beast. The water barrel was still attached to the bed of the wagon, but bone dry. There was a rope coiled up under the buckboard seat.

Titus and Mr. Whittacker, who both had backgrounds in black-smithing and wagon repair, carefully looked over the wagon. Other than de-vining it and some minor work, the wagon had actually been pretty well-protected from the elements by the vines. In the meantime, everyone else was clearing vines out of the way. I used this time to check on Jacob with Mrs. Robertson. His foot was much better, but he still had headaches if he walked on it. We changed his dressing and put a little more fat bacon on it before rewrapping it with clean wrapping and his own laundered socks.

Once the buckboard was cleaned up and the extra ox from the Lindes and the Rosses was hooked up and trailing behind the wagon, Mrs. Linde offered to drive the buckboard and to carry two of the Brahms children.

While making the offer to the Brahms, it was discovered that two of the Brahms girls, 12-year-old Rachael and 11-year-old Betsey, had both been walking the entire distance and had worn their shoes out. This caused a number of sore spots on their feet. The berry vine and the thorns had not helped. They would be riding with Mrs. Linde on the buckboard, which would be moved up to position 10 behind the Brahms. They would be great company for Mrs. Linde.

Brad talked with Dennis this morning about doing more shoe repair with some of his pelts. He was doing very little shod services since our oxen didn't wear shoes. But we sure were keeping him busy making shoes for our two-leggeds!

It was another hour or so before we were told to halt once again. Not from vines, but tracks, old wagon tracks. Because of the dirt and the rocks where we were, the tracks could have been a couple of weeks old, but they were not, because those vines couldn't have grown back that quickly. We were thinking the wagon passed by here some time ago. Could have been a couple of years, maybe even in '43, when the Applegate bunch were scouting the area. Either way, onward we went.

For two more hours, we pushed ourselves. Lots of changes today and little distance covered. I didn't figure we went any more than 10 miles with the time spent clearing berry vines, harvesting food, and finding and preparing a buckboard for travel along the way.

No signs of cat, deer, or bear today. It would be a vegetable diet tonight, with a sparse amount of cat left from last night and with the emphasis on light. But we had more fresh foods and a new buckboard to help take the load off.

Chapter Twenty

Last night, while supping with many, I had the opportunity to study some of our younger travelers. Although Titus Ross and Jesse Robertson were both as old as me, and Adam Parker and Will Robertson were pushing right behind, I felt much more mature—probably because of my being married and all. Of course, crossing the desert after my husband dying before my very eyes, out on a scorching flatland, didn't do much to remove the worry lines.

Titus had stood like a man and was now spoken for by Betha Robertson. They still had a bit of courting to do, but they had set their minds to it. Made me pretty sure there would be a wedding with this pair after we were all settled in the Oregon Territory.

Betha was a pretty girl with wavy blond hair and blue eyes the color of forget-me-nots. I overheard one traveler say she looked a little "highfalutin," but I knew from before that looks could be deceiving. She was solid and stuck by her decisions. She paid close attention to her dress and hair, but didn't dwell on it. She would make a good wife and mother.

Our dinner and dance last night brought several things to light. Will Robertson, a young man of 16, took time to get to know 15-year-old Trish Parker better. Will stood about 5'10" with a slender build. Not thin, nor frail looking, but sinuous-looking.

He moved smoothly and quietly. I also noticed that none of the Robertson men, including Joseph, the father, carried or partook in tobacco. I noticed that because many men had that habit. I looked first at the teeth, then for the tobacco pouch. So glad for their womenfolk that they did not have the chewing and spitting habit. It would have changed the look of Will if I had noticed such a custom. Nalan chewed, and I did my best to avoid his touch to my lips, although I did not keep him from his marital rights.

Will and Trish continued their easy and enjoyable friendship, nothing more at this point. *What a great blessing, to have friends each direction you turn.*

Trish was a weaver of baskets. The first one that I saw was a basket she made for her Mother Mary while she was carrying little Margaret; *may she rest in peace.* The carrier was not only durable, but beautiful. No better job could have been done by one of the resident natives.

Trish, even though only 15, had a beautiful heart. She listened well to what people said or didn't say. During the evening, she stored things, sometimes small, sometimes not, until she thought best to bring them forth, always in a healthy and helpful way. She was an old soul in a young person's body. Trish had glowing darker skin and dark hair mostly pulled back to a bun on the back of her neck. When I saw her on the trail, she was usually wearing a bonnet. She took pride in her appearance, which I was sure she learned from her Mother.

At Brad's request, Dennis had checked the shoes of several folks. He discovered that many were harboring achy, sore feet from the miles of walking. He used a string to measure the lengths of the feet for several of them, including Titus, who has been doing double duty walking with his patrolling back and forth and never riding.

Dennis said Titus and the Brahm sisters would be the first to receive new footwear. However, he said he expected people to speak up from now on. It was not good to wait until sores and open cuts were festering before saying something. It was much harder to treat open sores and infected feet than to keep them from getting that way.

Brad agreed and said each person was responsible to speak up, since checking shoes at night was not one of his wagon master duties.

In the meantime, Dennis filled the bottom sole of Titus' shoes with soft pieces of buckskin. He tacked the buckskin in with the smallest of deer gut thread. According to Titus, his feet laughed all the rest of the day from their newly-found comfort.

Rush Spencer called Brad to the front of his wagon and told him that he wanted to speak with him tonight when we settled. We were pretty sure it would be about the order of the lineup of the wagons. That would be fine with me.

I've been treated more than fairly on this trip and think others should be, too. Just keep the man away from me or next time I may stomp more than one foot. And what I don't stomp, I'm sure someone else will be glad to finish.

One of our other outriders, Ben, trotted up beside my wagon today and started a conversation. This was the first time I'd really spoken with him. With several chattering little children in my wagon, it was a little hard to hear at times, but I got the drift. He was sparking me. In the middle of the day!

"The gap between my top front teeth make it easier to whistle," he said with an impish grin. A bearded, decent-looking man, he was always funning with folks on the train. Mary Parker said he sometimes threw peppermint candies into her wagon when her little ones were there.

Now I knew why I'd been finding peppermint in the back of my wagon. Except for this morning, when I found four carved animal figures. My young passengers, two of the Parkers and two of the Robertson children, found them straight away and were delighted. The children had played non-stop with them since they climbed into the wagon.

I did notice a tobacco pouch hanging from Ben's belt. It didn't make any difference at this point, since the only one I'm interested in sparking with was Chase. Of course, I was not telling that to a soul. It would do Chase some good to fret that others were interested. I did enjoy visiting with Ben though, and he was a great help and solid traveling companion for all of us. Besides, it was still a little early to be thinking of another with Nalan not too long in his shallow desert grave.

But Chase continued to check on me, morning and night. He made himself available when preparing the animals early and late each day. He also checked on us periodically if we stopped during the day. I did as much as possible myself, knowing he was single and had his own rig. If I couldn't take responsibility, I should have turned back the day I buried Nalan.

While Ben and I were talking, I mentioned about finding the candy and the carved animals and asked him what his part in it was. He shared with me that he left home at a pretty young age, only 15 years and a few days old. He was part of a family with several younger children. They were very poor, and he being the oldest, the chores fell to him. His parents just kept having kids, but not improving their circumstances. He started carving toys so his brothers and sisters would have something to play with, or so that they could have a gift under the Christmas tree. He just never stopped carving or thinking about his young siblings. I told him that was very thoughtful of him to leave the carved animals in my wagon. It sure made the kids happy, and I was sure it did the same for his siblings back home.

The wagons groaned along with quiet voices coming from inside and alongside the wagons. Oxen still needed to be tapped with a quirt ever so often or taken by a rope and led. The bulky animals tended to walk with their heads down, looking at the ground rather than looking at the future in front of them.

It was so nice to have everyone with a traveling conveyance once again. The buckboard was smaller, but worked perfectly since the Ross family had lost most of their possessions when they lost their wagon. Buckboards were known for their flexibility and were considered the workhorse of any ranch, able to carry the family, groceries, or implements from one side of the ranch to the other.

In this case, the buckboard carried Mrs. Ross, what was left of her family belongings, and two of the Brahms girls, ages 11 and 12. It was pulled by one ox rather than a horse, but it was an appreciated change. Especially since the girls had been walking for such a long distance and their feet were quite sore. They would soon have new moccasins that Dennis was creating. The girls chatted off and on with Mrs. Ross, taking turns, with one or the other sitting up front on the buckboard seat, but mostly they stayed to themselves in the back of the buckboard.

They had some little game they played where they drew on each other's backs with their fingers and tried to guess what the other was drawing. It kept them happy and occupied. Just like Mrs. Ross, they did get tired of riding and wanted to do some walking, but Mrs. Ross assured them that it was best to wait until their new moccasins were on their feet. They, being well-behaved young girls, agreed and stayed put except for stops to relieve themselves.

Brad rode up and down the line today, making sure that everything was going smoothly. The tiredness and the monotony were starting to show on our company. Most of the physical problems were with sore feet and deep bramble scratches. Actually, some of these scratches were more like skin tears. They burned a bit too, according to some of the menfolk that thought they could tame them. These wounds were made before they discovered the machete.

I spent a lot of time thinking about what the end of the trail, at least for me, would look like. *How will I build my own place and take care of it?* I had a feeling that settling and living in the west would be much different than the east. I knew that I didn't want a huge place. I also didn't want to live miles from my neighbors. I hoped that some of these precious friends would also be my neighbors when we finally parked these wagons. I figured I needed a place with a little open space, but close to trees that could be cut for building and to keep a nice winter fire going in my home.

I kept hearing chickens squawking today. I asked Brad where the sounds were coming from. He said one of the company, about midway back, Delia and Jack McCall and their two daughters, had not only several chickens, but also a cow tied to the back of their wagon. Their laying hens got pretty excited sometimes and, depending on what kind of territory we were in, their noise carried more than other times. He said when they had an abundance, the McCalls occasionally shared their eggs with those folks closest to them.

He said they also had butter and milk. I was surprised to hear that they hang their milk bucket with cream in it under the wagon, and it has enough movement to "churn" itself as we traveled throughout the day. That was on flatter ground, of course, so as not to spill or lose the bucket. Good to know. They sounded very enterprising.

Tonight, I will make a point of walking back and introducing myself. Funny that I heard the chickens and was thinking about what the squawking was all about today. It was time to meet everyone on the train, and this was a great conversation to start with. I was sure that those that I have not met have a story to tell along with their dreams for the future. Possibly it would be good to ask Mary to take a walk with me so that she could meet some of the other folks, too.

We were traveling where others had traveled previously. Today as I went delicately into the brush to relieve myself, I spotted a small, round end-table, lightweight with a bottom shelf on it. Made well, but left behind just the same. I loaded it into my wagon along with a cane-back chair. I figured I could carry them as long as it made sense. Once we reached our destination, I would have something to start my new life, or I would use them to barter for something I needed. *Who knows?* The buckboard that we found earlier may have belonged to the same group of earlier settlers. I had to be aware that I had to keep room for little travelers and not fill up my wagon with remnants of another train.

Chase spent an awful amount of time during the day by himself. He seemed all right with it. In fact, when I saw him as wagons stopped for the night or for a respite, he was ready on the mark with a smile and an exchange of conversation. He was so helpful and positive, and I couldn't help but think how nice it would be if he were in my life when we got situated further north. In fact, I found myself fantasizing about how life could be with a man like Chase by my side.

As I sat here on the wagon seat, I realized that the wagons in front had stopped, and there seemed to be some activity over to the right side of the trail. I halted my oxen with a pull on the reins. Someone yelled and a shot was fired, then another. I quickly turned my head to the children.

"Lay down in the wagon and be very quiet!" I ordered. They did. Young children on the prairie were taught to listen and obey when ordered. Sometimes it was a matter of life and death.

The activity slowed as quickly as it escalated. We would have venison tonight for dinner. Adam Parker had just shot a deer, and Mr. Parker shot a second one. It seemed that a couple of deer were interested in the passersby and the unfamiliar site of wagons. They became our dinner without much fanfare. They were tasty and much appreciated.

Brad called Dennis, Rocky, and Ben to the side of the train and asked them to start dressing out the pair of deer. We had more distance to make yet today, but couldn't leave the deer all day without dressing them out and preparing for dinner tonight. The deer were both a decent size, so they were quartered up and disbursed up and down the wagon line so that dinner pots would be ready to put on the fire when they stopped for the evening. Dennis was also taking the hides to make moccasins and whatever else he might need.

While the deer were being dressed, cut up, and disbursed, I got out a couple of jars, poured vinegar into them, added clean wild onions, and sealed the jar. Sometimes it was easier to get folks to eat a pickled vegetable rather than taking vinegar as a daily supplement. I was going to keep reminding folks that it was an easy way to combat scurvy.

Being on this wagon train had been a big learning experience. You prepared for the unseen. You found moments of time to complete what seemed like a small task at that time. However, it could make a big difference down the road. You made yourself available to others because you could, and because they were your neighbors trying to get to their dreams with their family intact just like you were.

And so, I did what I could with every spare moment, unabashedly and with an open heart.

Several hours later, with heavy legs on walkers and tongues lolling from the oxen, we came to a spot that Dennis and Brad agreed on. It was at the foot of a mountain, heavily treed. A creek ran nearby. Small but cool with somewhat clear water. Enough for watering the animals, bathing, and washing the dust out of our clothes, depending on the amount of energy you had left, and what amount of effort you wanted to expend.

The young men laid the fires for cooking as their fathers saw to the animals and wagons, carefully checking the feet, of the oxen. Once they had completed that task, the men went to the river to clean up. In the meantime, the women were putting the pots on for fresh venison stew. Onions, sage, and mushrooms were added. A few had mushrooms, or dried squash, cut into much smaller pieces and thrown in. Not many though, since food was exhausting quickly.

Then the women made a trip to the creek. Little ones first, so their Moms could get them cleaned up and delivered back for watching over by their Pas or an older sibling. Then we had about 15 minutes prior to everyone wanting to eat. We were hungry. Most of the adults had not had anything all day except for maybe a bite of hardtack for breakfast. The children were fed in the mornings and given something to chew on as the day progressed to keep their young, flat stomachs from growling.

Within an hour or so, aromas rose from the pots, setting everyone's mouths to watering. I had a chance to rinse out my shawl and one of my undergarments while bathing. It would feel good to start with at least some clean clothes tomorrow.

Dinner was quiet as everyone ate heartily of venison stew. There was plenty to fill all the pots, and what was left was stored in containers for tomorrow's dinner. It was nice to know where our next meal was coming from.

During our bathing time, I asked Mary if after dinner she would like to take a walk with me to meet some of the other folks, especially the McCalls. I was real curious about their chickens and their cow. I wanted to know how they were faring, and if the animals were calm enough to actually deliver eggs and milk as they did before they started on the trip.

Mary was delighted that I had asked her and quickly agreed. After dinner, we left Trish and Adam in charge of helping with the cleanup of dinner. We made sure that Ned Parker knew that he had little Nikolus to care for if he got fussy, as well as watching over five-year-old Jeremiah and Tom, who was four. Ned was happy to oblige, knowing that Mary never got away from all of her children at one time. The walk and meeting other folks would be good for her.

We walked down the line with young Titus doing a slow walk in front of us. He had his rifle loaded and was constantly at attention. He would make a good military man. Titus spoke to several as he walked down the line. When appropriate, he introduced me and Mary to others. As we were being introduced, we had an opportunity to see each family's different types of setups. There were as many different setups as there were families. When we got to the halfway mark, we met the McCalls. Chickens, cow, girls, and all.

They had just pulled the bucket of cream, which was now butter, from beneath the wagon. The day's journey had rocked and churned it into a tasty, creamy, spreadable butter. Salt was all that was missing. They were gathering the eggs from the laying hens. Two roosters filled cages, as well as eight laying hens in a separate cage. There was not any room left in the back of their Conestoga. They also had a four-up hitch of oxen to pull with.

They started with 1,200 pounds of food, plus double the original amount suggested for the animals, since they had four oxen and a larger, heavier wagon. Each night they said they pulled a tarp from the top of their wagon's wooden sides and anchored it to the ground. Mr. and Mrs. McCall slept there, while the girls slept inside the wagon where quarters were warmer, although tighter.

The chicken and rooster cages were roped to the outside of the wagon with heavy tarps over the top and wrapped, so no animals could access them at night. The tarps also kept it darker so the rooster didn't start crowing in the middle of the night during a full moon.

It was obvious to both Mary and me that it was extra work to bring along more animals. We asked the McCalls if they thought it was worth it. Both of them heartily agreed that it was worth it for several reasons. The number of eggs that they got each day made a significant difference in their diets and what they could cook. Also, they were happy to have milk for their young children's growing bodies.

They said it was hard work for the whole family. The girls, 12-year-old Olivia and 13-year-old Meg, were expected to help with the caring of the animals. In fact, that was their job: to feed and water the oxen and cow every day, both morning and night. To feed the fowl and harvest their eggs and to milk the cow. Mr. McCall would put the bucket of cream under the wagon when they made butter. The McCalls made a pretty attractive point when they mentioned that eggs were great protein when meat was not available. Besides, if a hen quit laying, she could quickly be made into dinner. Although they hadn't had to do that yet! The family menu was much larger than those folks that didn't have eggs or milk. When Mrs. McCall made biscuits, they came with freshly-made, creamy butter.

As it started to get darker, Titus reminded us that we should get back to our wagons. We shook hands and hugged Mrs. McCall and the girls, thanking them for the hot biscuit, slathered with melting fresh butter and started to step away when Mrs. McCall asked us to wait. At which point, she and her oldest handed me a bowl of eggs. There were at least a dozen large, fresh eggs. Mary and I expressed our elation with wide smiles and a big thank you. As we headed back to our wagons, we made plans about what to fix for breakfast tomorrow, using our eggs, of course.

It was pretty quiet by the time we got back. Small children had been tucked away for the night. A night watch had been set up. Once again, we were not far from the creek, which could be a water source for the local four-leggeds. We needed to be prepared in case any unfriendlies show up.

"Want to sit for a spell and visit?" Chase asked.

I was more than happy to spend some time with him. He handed me a dipper of water and we sat on a log next to the fire. It was our time to let ourselves learn to be comfortable with each other and to talk about our dreams. I shared my fears with Chase, being single and all, and wondering how I was going to settle in once we reached our destination.

"Don't borrow problems," Chase said with an assuring tone. "I'm single, too, but I have a good suspicion that I found my dream, and that we'll work together to settle our new home in the west."

He left no question about who or what that dream was.

Chapter Twenty-One

The night had crept in quietly and left a sharp, icy morning. The significant drop in temperature left us all digging for warmer garments. Cold mist blanketed the air, and the day promised to be quiet and long. Today I decided I'd be wearing my black felt hat pulled down instead of a bonnet, which was more suited to keeping the sun off than keeping the head warm and dry.

As I rolled out of my nest, I remembered that we had something to look forward to: eggs for breakfast! What a treat. As our little "unit" got up next to the fire, we handed each a small portion of eggs to go with their coffee, or with tea for the children. There were plenty of smiles all around.

The eggs were delicious. Everyone savored the scramble, loaded with wild onions and a few diced-up mushrooms. It was amazing how starting out with a comfortable belly was making the day look mighty fine, even in the cold with a threat of rain. Everyone was so appreciative of the change in the diet and actually getting some breakfast.

I noted again this morning that coffee and tea supplies were getting very low. I suggested to Brad that we not offer coffee during our rest stops. It made more sense to save it for mornings and evenings only. That would also make those meals, when we had them, more filling.

I ended up wearing my long, canvas coat most of the day, as did others. It not only kept any breeze out, but also kept everything dry. It was also a good stop against any tree branches or berry brambles we would pass through. The coat was great when I was standing still, but tended to force my dress close around my legs, and that sometimes made it harder to prevent bushes from catching and tearing at the bottom of my skirt. On flat ground, I could drive from the seat of the wagon, and it wasn't so much of a problem, but when I was leading the oxen or walking alongside the wagon for safety purposes, I knew every bush on the trail intimately as my skirt got tangled in it.

We stopped about two hours down the trail as the incline was getting steeper and dense with brush. Brad told everyone to take a break. He suggested we check our wagons, again, especially the brakes and wheels. There was some rock going up the hill, but for the most part, the trail was pretty much non-existent, or at least there was no true sign of it. We were finding that wasn't uncommon. Sometimes it seemed like a well-marked path would just simply disappear within 10 feet of a trail. If it were rocky, much of it had to do with hard-packed dirt or a powdery soil. There wasn't a whole lot of the powdery soil.

It also had something to do with wagon trains splitting up and going in different directions. By this time on the trail, many of the settlers were getting tired of each other. Their bodies were worn, and they were hungry. All very similar to how we were beginning to feel. Each settler was thinking maybe he could make better decisions than the wagon master.

We are fortunate so far. I believe that we have good, strong leaders within our group of 20 wagons. For the most part, everyone was working together. We had a good combination of skillful people to believe in and trust, who made our lives a bit more comfortable.

Speaking of skillful. Dennis was probably one of the most resourceful folks traveling with us. This morning, before we broke camp, he showed us a wooden trap that he had worked on the evening before. He said that he felt this was a good area to scare up some sage hens. Tonight, after we were stationary, he would set them.

Something else that he did surprised me. He took some deer gut that he used for sewing or wrapping his traps together and went to visit Rush Spencer. He gave the deer gut to Rush after showing him his cage and suggested, in a very non-confrontational way, that he, Rush, build a trap as well. Rush seemed very happy with the idea and took the deer gut. Dennis believed Rush caused problems because he didn't feel needed. If he could help with the food source on his end of the train, it would certainly make a difference. *We shall see if he rises to the occasion.*

Dennis had also finished Rachael's moccasins and gave them to her last night. You would have thought it was Christmas. They fit like they were made for her. Probably because they were! Betsy, her sister, was concerned that Dennis had forgotten her. He assured her that her moccasins would be done that night if nothing else came up. She knew that he was not much of a talker, so when he said something, he meant it. The girls were excited about being able to walk again, at least for a short distance each day. They would have to walk. Especially when we started up or went down some of the steeper grades we saw before us.

Not to make the young boys feel left out, Dennis took materials and a finished slingshot that he had made down to the Wiggins wagon and spoke to 16-year-old Tanner. He gave Tanner the finished sling and some deer gut. He explained how to make the slingshot and told him he would be in charge of helping the other boys learn how to make slings, starting with Jacob Robertson and including the five-year-old boys. He suggested to Tanner that he let him know when they each had a piece of wood to carve. At that time, he would give them instructions on how to make a working handle for accuracy and how to shoot at a target. Hopefully, one with meat to fill their bellies.

I took the opportunity to walk with Dennis to the Wiggins wagon to speak with the mister's 14-year-old daughter, Kate. As I mentioned before, she was educated and her and her brother Tanner had some very invigorating discussions. Her intelligence and book learning were most impressive. I talked to her, after speaking first with Mr. Wiggins, of course, about the possibility of her teaching other children on the trail. He would have to be supportive of her, since she had her own responsibilities in camp at night, such as cooking. Tanner joined the conversation and told us that he would be more helpful so that she would not be overly taxed.

Kate was very surprised, but smiled openly and showed her interest. Together we decided that once we have crossed this mountain range, school would begin each day after our dinner. It would include an hour each night, or as long or as short as we had light. All the children, including and especially the teens, would get daily instruction. The first night would be to assess how much education each child already had, starting with the alphabet and reading and writing their own names.

Brad was in favor and full of smiles at the possibility of his settlers being educated in more ways than one on this trip.

We wondered how much weight the oxen could pull as we prepared for what was ahead. We wondered even more about how much they could keep off their backsides going down the grades. That was where the trouble could really start. If the oxen couldn't pull going uphill because the load was simply too heavy or because they were worn out from all the miles, they just stopped. In some rare cases, they could be pulled backwards, but not often. However, they didn't have that choice if the weight was on their backsides. Besides having to find their way, they had all that weight pushing them from behind. It was a definite recipe for tragedy or, at the minimum, a way to wear out oxen. On a wagon train, that was a tragedy.

We knew that when we started the steep terrain, folks would be walking again. Sometimes holding a rope tied to the wagon in order to lessen the weight on the oxen's backside, and sometimes helping by pushing on the sides of the wagon going uphill. Folks, young and old alike, would have to be adaptable and aware.

Having strong leaders, such as our wagon master Brad, was very important. He spotted troubles before they began. Hopefully.

Young Jacob Robertson was feeling much better. His foot sores had finally healed and his headaches had abated. With his new pair of moccasins, and being thoroughly healed (and bored according to him), he was prepared to do his share of walking again. In fact, he was looking forward to it.

It would be tough getting all the little ones out of the wagons and on foot again, but they had to walk in these mountains in case a wagon got loose. I trusted that they would do what needed to be done. They had so far. These children were tough. But they also needed affection and good words directed at them to feed their little souls. *God bless them all.*

According to a sparse map that Brad had, and near as Dennis could figure with his scouting, we would soon be next to the Rogue River. This was the territory of the Rogue Indians, which thus far we had not seen hide nor hair of. We had not heard any stories, good or bad, about them, either. Of course, we hadn't come across any folks since we left the Fort some time ago. There was some talk about crossing the Rogue River. Mostly it was just stories of single riders crossing by holding onto the tails of their horses as they swam across. Some called a camp next to the crossing Tailholt.

We still had to make it up and over this steep hill before we were down within easy distance of the river. According to the map, the hillside looked like the spine of the backside of one of our oxen: uneven and long. We didn't know if it would take one day or several days, but we were preparing, like soldiers going to war. We were settlers aiming for a better life, and we were certainly not ready to give up. Not yet, anyway.

As we readied for our ascent, Mothers were tying shoes so that their children's shoelaces didn't trip them up at a critical time. They had made sure that all had on their warmest coat and that each was carrying their own canteen of water in case a wagon got loose and lost a water barrel. Even though we would soon be next to a river, they were not taking any chances. The older boys were carrying their rifles, always at the ready for the unknown.

I had even noticed the increased amount of personal touches and conversations between married couples today as we prepared for our ascent of the mountain. I would be driving my own wagon up the hill. There would be discussion as to who would drive it downhill once we had made it to the summit and saw what was before us. I didn't have as much driving experience as most of the men. Coming down a steep hillside with wagons afore and behind was not the best place to learn.

Wagon wheel chocks were placed accessible on the seats of each wagon so the driver could toss them down or one of the older boys walking on the left side of the wagons could grab them. When we stopped, chocks would always be used, both up and down the hillsides.

Brad talked with me in private today and shared that once we were across the mountain in front of us, he would be switching our lineup, depending on how everything went. "I'm ready for that," I said. "I have no issue."

Since I had arrived late on this train, I had been treated very well and expected to be under the same direction as everyone else. He should do what was best for everyone. *I have no worries that Brad will do what is fair. I am hoping, however, that Chase will be somewhere close by in our new lineup.* I was wondering why he brought this subject up just before this trip up the hill, and I thought I figured it out. He was trying to take my mind off this hill that we were facing.

I must say, he has divided my fears; therefore, he has been somewhat successful. I guess that's why he's the wagon master.

I did have the opportunity to talk with Chase last night and again this morning as we readied my team, and we shared a smile and eye contact over breakfast. He was very supportive about the idea of the Wiggins girl teaching the children. He mentioned that there might be an opportunity for some of the adults to also get some schooling. He said he knew of a couple of adults further back in the train that could use some help learning to read and write. He also suggested if there was interest from the adults that it might be a good time to get Tanner involved, too, being that he was older than Kate, and probably further educated than his sister. If Tanner were so inclined.

I couldn't help myself when I said, "Wouldn't it be nice if people could sign their homestead claims and actually know what they're signing?" I could see my dreams getting clearer, and they didn't include just me.

"Load up" carried down the line from one wagon to another. It seemed almost immediately that "wagons ho" melted into my being. And with a snap of whips up and down the line, we started to move. "Locks, step out." Children walked beside the wagon under the watchful eyes of their mother, staying far enough from the wagon so as not to get caught under a metal wheel or get lost in the shrubbery. Mothers carried their wee ones, and the older children held the hands of younger siblings and pulled them up the hillsides.

It was slow going. I sat high on the wagon seat with a wheel chock on the seat next to me. We were to stay on the trail that Dennis and Brad scouted for us, but stagger our positions. I constantly spoke to Nellie and Locks, my pair of oxen. They were doing their best, even with less food each day. The four little ones did not weigh much. I was sure my oxen appreciated the lighter weight as they trudged up the hillside, occasionally stumbling over rocks and large branches rutted in the ground.

"Nellie and Locks," I ordered gently but firmly, "keep going." They reacted quietly as I guided them to stagger the position of the wagon in front of me. The wagons serpentined up the hill. As I looked around the left side of my wagon cover, I saw the wagon behind me and two-wagon-lengths back.

Should one of the wagons roll backwards, we didn't want the wagons behind it to catch it or for it to run over someone. All of our young children were walking on the right side of the ascending wagons next to their mothers or older sisters who weren't driving a team. The young men were on the left side carrying a loaded rifle or a chock in their arms, ready for fast action.

With wagons spread out and stretching down the hill, Brad stayed busy on his horse, going back and forth checking on folks, leaving Dennis to lead the wagons through the best route of the trail, what there was of it.

I had put together some hardtack this morning before breaking camp. I gave it to the mothers to give to their children as they saw fit. The little ones were much more apt to walk without complaining if their energy stayed up. Mary carried baby Nikolus in her arms while five-year-old Jeremiah, and Tom, who was just four years old, hung onto their sister Trish, a very grown-up young lady of 15. She was uncomplaining and consistent with her treatment of her younger siblings and always looking after their safety and how she could assist her Mother.

Five-year-old Sarah Robertson held the hand of her 12-year-old sister Clara as they maneuvered the hillside. Their Mother, Anna, was walking with them, as was their 15-year-old sister, Emily. Will and Jesse, 15 and 18 respectively, managed the team from the ground. Their dad, Joseph, drove from the wagon seat. They had a Conestoga with a four-up of oxen. It took more effort, time, and feed for that type of wagon setup. It was sorely needed for the family of 10.

All those walking had to be reminded, often, to keep their eyes upward to see what the wagons were doing ahead of looking down at the ground one step ahead of them like our beasts of burden, the oxen, do.

It was a long, full day, but Dennis said he thought our first wagon would soon reach the place where the trail would level out for a bit. We needed everyone on level ground tonight, before dark, and before we set up camp. We rolled on, jerking over bumps and potholes for another 45 minutes before Dennis stopped the Gills in the first wagon. They were followed by the Parkers. About the time Chase was staggering his wagon, Brad came trotting up to tell me to stay on my wagon seat, once I was parked, until he told me otherwise. He would tell Chase to chock my wheels as well as assist the Robertson family in front of me. He said there was a little activity at the back of the train that he was going to see finished before we would actually set up camp.

Finally, all the wagons were up the hill, stationary, and chocked for safety. I was free to climb down. It appeared that a rabbit had raced across the path in front of the Tanner Wiggins wagon and spooked the oxen a mite. Tanner, as smooth as you please, pulled out his sling shot that Dennis had given him this morning and let a small rock fly. His shot was true. He had furnished the protein for his dinner tonight, and for the dinner of his traveling companions.

The buckboard that Mrs. Ross was driving, being pulled by a single ox, needed a little help on the last part of the hill climb. Mrs. Ross drove while Titus and Mr. Ross pushed from behind.

Lots of conversation tonight. Tanner Wiggins and his travel group, including the Brahms, McCall, and Linde families, would do as they had been and share their meal with everyone contributing something. Once they got parked, the ladies put on a pot and started the dried vegetables while Tanner skinned the rabbit for the stewpot. It was a small portion for each because of the number of folks sharing the pot, but it was a dinner filled with smiles. They made it through the first day, and Tanner's first shot with his sling went true to the mark.

Even before all the wagons had made it to the top of the hill, Dennis and "the boys" were headed out to rope off an area to "corral the animals." A highline rope for the few horses was strung as close to grass as manageable. The oxen were in the same area, but were hobbled so as to move in a small space. The horses were hobbled as well as being on a line. Horses tended to chew on the wagons or could pull one crooked. Again, it was taking those extra precautions that would get us to "Eden" intact.

Dennis, once finished with the horse and ox corral, came back from setting his trap for the sage hens and shared that an unmarked grave sat less than 50 feet from our front camp. The ground was too hard to dig, so a very shallow grave showed because it was piled with rocks to protect the carcass from animals and weather.

Lying beside the grave was a neatly folded smock and worn women's boots, soles hanging, and tear marks from prior brambles. Alone, windblown, and sun-scarred, just like the body in the unnamed grave. We deduced that it was a woman's grave. After dinner, several of us visited the grave. Without touching or disturbing it in any way, we prayed over her for peace in her next life, and for the rest of us struggling forth.

Chapter Twenty-Two

THE GRAVE WE PRAYED over was not the only one we found. More unmarked graves dotted the top of the hill, along with assorted pieces of furniture, a heavy skillet, and extra clothing. It was as if those who crossed before us were reinforcing the importance of lightening our loads before, rather than after, crossing mountains if you wanted to be sure it was not the last mountain you climbed. Most of the belongings we found were not touched or loaded into our wagons, regardless of room. Near void clothing was laid on the ground with only bones sticking from the sleeves and pants. Rocks were piled in an attempt to keep the body from being further desecrated. No remaining food was found.

At this point of our journey, dreams keep us moving forward, though riddled with sadness for those who didn't make it. It was clear that without our dreams, we could not crawl up and over mountains, float and swim across rivers, camp in alkali flats and, of course, eat a supper of dirt served up with coffee, no longer strong. Dreams remained because of our new friends, all pioneers with guts who wanted a new and better life.

We knew that up to this point of our travels, settlers died from accidents, snakebites, disease, and depending on your location, Indian attacks (of which we have had none to date). Hardships didn't always come in big events. It was the daily grind of walking for 10 hours a day behind a wagon that was blowing dust back in your face, pulling your skirts from berry vines, finding a place to go to the bathroom in private while on the desert. It was having a toothache and no powders to help with the pain, or feet blistered and sore because there was no Dennis to make you a new pair of shoes. It was every day of every month for five or six months without a break that caused pioneers to lose their drive and sometimes their mind. It caused them, like oxen, to STOP. Right where they stood or fell down. Sometimes to shed some tears before getting back up, other times lifted up by their fellow travelers. Taking turns keeping each other strong, or at the very least, moving.

Folks were quiet tonight after supping light. I figured most were congenial rather than wasting effort on arguing. We were waiting for the conversation between Rush Spencer and Brad to finish. We were pretty confident that we would get a new wagon lineup once we get over this hill tomorrow or the next day.

In the meantime, I discovered that Dennis had paid a visit to Betsy this morning. Thank goodness it was before we started up the hill. True to his word, he had completed the moccasins for her sore feet. Betsy was so excited once she had them on and felt their comfort. He had padded the bottoms well, so as not to have the rocks bruising her feet. She said it was like having the protection of hard-soled shoes, except they were also soft and felt like her feet were being caressed. Others were now even more excited about learning to make moccasins themselves when the life in their own shoes was "all walked out."

Skills would help to get us to the end of the trail, whether that be "Eden" or some other place further north. Having skillful people on the trip to teach others was a real blessing. As soon as we got back to some level ground, our schooling would start for reading, writing, and numbers. Dennis would also be taking some time out to show the boys how to make and use their slings. In addition he would teach Rush, and any other interested folks, how to make wooden traps. He was including women in that. As if they didn't already have a full plate.

I found it was not just about educating folks, which was very important; it was about getting and keeping their minds on a positive track. Helping them to forget that we have exhausted much of our food supply, including food for our animals. The animals were worn out and moving slower with each passing day. Without them we couldn't survive.

We were gathering our dreams and resources and sharing with each other, which made some folks angry. It was frustrating for those who took the time to plan and bring reserves of food for both themselves and their animals, only to share with those who planned little, ran out early, and were now eating reserves from someone else's supply. It was a big irritation to almost everyone that Brad constantly had to monitor. Tempers flared easily.

Some wagon trains didn't share their food when supplies ran low. Others, like ours, left it up to their teamsters to make that decision as long as the food lasts. Most teamster families chose to share with a couple of wagons in front and behind if the sharing was equal. On this trip, we were in groups of five wagons. I didn't know how I would say to the Parker family, or any other family, "I will not share my food with your beautiful and hungry child." For me, it was a decision of my heart, not a figure in a ledger, saying that I furnished two squash and a pan of biscuits when a family was only able to share one squash. However, I had been fortunate to be paired with folks who were more than fair.

Earlier when I mentioned the workload of the women on the trip, I was thinking of everything that she had to do, most of the time with a baby in her arms and expecting another. Many of the families were smaller, mostly because the man was traveling without a woman. In the instances of a husband and wife, the average family was eight to 10 children. That meant that the mother's job was keeping track of all those children. That was in addition to cooking, cleaning up the camp, picking fresh food along the trail, doing laundry when water was available, helping take care of the animals, and, of course, keeping her husband happy.

Hopefully, there were older children that could help with the chores and managing the smaller ones. That took a big load off the parents. The Parker and Robertson families were examples of that situation working really well.

While we were setting up our camps tonight, Emily Robertson and Trish Parker, both 15, and Clara Robertson, 12, combined their efforts and collected acorns and pine cones, all within sight of our camp to ensure their safety. The acorns would be shucked with the outside shells taken off, then dried, and the nuts inside ground. We wouldn't eat the acorns right away since they had to be dried before they were made into flour. The pine nuts were harvested from the pine cones of the pinyon pine trees. Pine cones had to be heartily shaken to remove the nuts. The cones were pitchy, some more than others, and could be quite messy. But the nuts were sweet, yet mild, buttery tasting with a hint of pine and quite substantial for energy and vitamins. It was a great way to extend food resources, even though it took a lot of them because of their size.

We were keeping in mind that the young ladies who picked the nuts were from large families with lots of mouths to feed. It was up to them to decide to share with others or to keep the benefits of their harvest for their own families. I suggested that they keep their first gathering for their own families. We would have more pine and acorn trees to share, at least for a couple more days. Everyone should have been helping to harvest since it was a ready source of food.

Speaking of food, Meg and Olivia McCall, along with their Mother Delia, showed up at the Parkers wagon tonight with half a dozen eggs and a small pail of milk. They said that they still had eggs and milk from the prior day that their family of four could not consume and wanted to share. Even though they apologized for it being such a small contribution, it was mentioned that with hot coffee or tea a bit of milk was perfect.

Mary Parker glowed as she said they would boil the eggs and the children could have them for tomorrow. The McCall ladies visited for 20 minutes or so before heading back to their wagon as the sun was setting down the mountainside. Trish Parker had already started a pot for boiling the eggs. Adam Parker, gun at the ready and without being asked, escorted the ladies back to their wagon.

I hadn't seen much of Rocky and Ben, but knew that they were never far. They kept us rounded up, helped move us safely up and down mountains and across streams and rivers. Most importantly, they watched for wild animals and two-leggeds, good and bad. What I didn't expect from them was their ability to build things or the soft spot in their hearts that they had for their fellow travelers. I should have known better, especially after my talk with Ben some time back.

He was a carver, so that should have told me he was a man with imagination and heart. Those gravesites that we had seen were unmarked with an actual cross. Ben made sure each one of them had one before we left the next morning. Normally we would leave the graves unmarked, if they were buried and hidden, but these were not. Now they were marked with the Christian cross, as if they had been buried in the ground in a fancy casket with family and friends in bowed acknowledgement.

I would be remiss by not mentioning Titus Ross. He came on this trip with his aunt and uncle, but had become a "foot soldier." Really, the young man was constantly watching out for all of us. On foot, gun loaded, and always ready for anything. Then, of course, he and Betha Robertson were a perfect match. It was delightful to watch their romance blossom.

Ours was a busy camp tonight. Brad went to see Rush, but first he had rabbit stew at the Wiggins camp with the mister, and his children, Tanner and Kate. Tanner had shot the rabbit this afternoon while settling into camp. Just in time to skin it and throw it in a pot for dinner. At 14 years old, his sister Kate had become a good hand around a cook pot. She added wild onions, mushrooms and sage for flavor and fixed a pan of biscuits to go with it. They even had a little butter that the McCalls had shared with them at an earlier meal.

While Brad visited, he told them there would be some placement changes in the train. He would share that with everyone once they came off the hill in a day or two. Brad thanked them for the dinner and the conversation and headed to the end of the train where Rush Spencer drove his wagon.

When Brad arrived, Rush was working on the trap using the plans and some deer-gut thread that Dennis had given him. He seemed really intent on his project, which calmed Brad a bit. The first months of the train Rush had been a pain to travel with, especially when harassing the womenfolk. That was why he had been threatened and placed at the back end of the train. Watching for uninvited guests kept him occupied. Between that and working on the trap, he was a little easier to talk to now.

Tonight, he had finished the trap and was actually trying to find the right food to tantalize an animal to walk into it. He was ready to set it out in hopes of having something edible by tomorrow morning.

Brad and Rush talked about the trap, Rush's food reserves, which like everyone else's were getting low, and how he was feeling about the journey. He made a few remarks meant to cut Brad, but Brad ignored it and began the process of talking to him about his responsibilities if he were moved up in the train. Brad assured him that he was going to have a big family in front of him and one directly behind him. He would be expected to help keep them moving ahead. This was the best part. Brad told him that he would be expected to help them in a kind and respectful manner without yelling, touching, or threatening them. If he were unable to do that, he would immediately go to the end of line or be expelled from the wagon train entirely because he had already used up two warnings.

Rush stuttered and stammered as Brad recounted the expectations, but he agreed. Rush would take the fourth position, right behind Mrs. Linde and in front of the Brahms family. That meant that most meals, depending on the others in the first five wagons, would share their dining pots and campfires, unless he chose to cook his own meals, at which point he was still expected to help the wagons move forward as needed.

During Brad's walk back to the front of the train, with a fresh biscuit in his coat pocket, he stopped off at a couple of other camps to speak with folks.

Amos Gode was two wagons away from Rush and the first stop Brad made after leaving Rush. Amos was working for his passage on the trail driving a "supply wagon" for Brad on behalf of the entire company. In a specially-built buckboard, he held troughs used for linseed to keep the wheels oiled. He also carried extra feed for oxen, a water barrel, materials to replace brakes on wagons, and other maintenance tools in anticipation that not everyone would have these "suggested items."

Amos had his 12-year-old nephew Calvin with him. He had taken custody of and cared for the young man two years prior when his Ma had passed away during childbirth and his Pa lost his mind and had run off and left him. Amos treated the boy very well and was extremely fond of him. Amos's wife had died just last year so he and Calvin were going for a fresh start.

Amos did not have the price to purchase a wagon, needing to save what cash he had for when they got to Oregon to set up their home. He had answered a post on the bulletin board at the general store in Fort Hall about a month before the company of settlers was to leave the Fort. The ad read:

> **Looking for Teamster to drive wagon to the Oregon Territory. In exchange for you driving the wagon, your passage will include a scout familiar with the route. Must be able to handle 4-up oxen, cook your own meals, help with wagons, wild Indians, and sickness. Contact wagon master Brad Trape at Mister Lou's Rooming House. Leave in one month.**

Amos found Brad, and the discussion ensued after Amos made plain that Calvin was included in the agreement and went where he went. Brad and Amos worked together to outfit the wagon with a special heavy-duty undercarriage. Calvin helped to apply pitch under the wagon for flotation. Wheels were well greased and serviced. They also built specially-designed troughs that were narrow and deep for the linseed oil to soak wheels while out on the trail. Knowing that they would not be able to travel the entire distance without maintenance.

Extra brake pads were made for more than one type and size of wagon in an attempt to anticipate what others were going to forget.

The wagon carried a large, heavily paraffined barrel. Calvin had helped his Uncle Amos with it. It carried linseed oil to be used on any wagon wheels needing it.

Wagon wheels were made from wood with a metal band around the outside of them. As wheels aged from time and the elements, the wood shrunk and left a space between the wood and the band. That made for a perfect time for the wagon wheels to break, or in some cases, for the spokes to fall out. Linseed oil helped to prevent the shrinkage. A large container that a wheel could be set in and left for an undisclosed time swelled that part of the wheel. The wheel was turned and the process for the next third or fourth of the wheel began, depending on the size of the trough being used. This was not a fast process and needed level ground and manpower to lift the wagon, remove the wheel, and reinstall it.

Amos and Calvin were invested in the trip and looking forward to moving on to their new life. They carried their own food stores and added extra. Brad ate with other settlers along the way as part of their agreement.

Brad, Calvin, Amos, and Solomon Whittacker sat around the campfire and discussed what Brad wanted to happen once they were on level ground. He had gotten word from Dennis that we would be on the mountain another full day, start down the second day, and hopefully safe and leveled out by midday.

Brad wanted to use that short day to work on the wagons. The rocks had played havoc with the wheels, and he was not entirely sure how much more some of the wagons could take. The wagons were different types, sizes, and weights. He didn't know how well everyone maintained their own wagon and did not want any of them to break down. Winter was pressing, and it was already showing frost in the mornings.

Once we made it to flat ground and they completed their wagons, Amos, Calvin, and Solomon would prepare to start at the back of the train and work their way to the front. Brad would check all wagons first and let them know which ones needed a good soaking. Brad had four troughs in the wagon. Enough to do all four wheels on a wagon at one time, then turn the wheel, and do them again. There were others who had their own troughs and oil and had done recent soakings. They would be helpful to the others in the train by helping them complete the soaking of their wheels.

Tomorrow night, Brad would be checking brake pads before starting down the mountain. Any that needed to be replaced would be done then. Until then we needed to be mindful and watch for anything awry.

Brad also filled in Amos that they would be moving up more to the middle of the train when we changed places on level ground. Solomon had shown to be handy with wood as a builder. He had built his own wagon and his own cabin back in Missouri. He was traveling alone, but looking forward to starting a construction business in Oregon. Brad quickly chose him to look over brake pads tomorrow night and replace any that need work before we start downhill.

Solomon Whittacker, 21, was quiet but not shy. He had thick, dark hair and eyes, was broad-shouldered, and was neat in his appearance, even though he was eating more than his share of dirt stirred up from those in front of us.

A conversation took place between all of them as to whether Solomon had someone special that would be joining him in Oregon once he settled in. He explained that he had a woman back home in Missouri. She refused to leave her parents and an area already "settled and civilized," as she put it, to traipse off to the "wild west on a wagon." Solomon stated that the answer to their question was no, no one special would be joining him.

By the time Brad got back to the front of the train, it was past dark. He crawled into his lean-to tent with a bedroll and extra canvas under him to scare off the cold night that already had come visiting.

Chase had stuck around the campfire making sure there was nothing more that he could do to help me. The Parker and Robertson families were trying to get their bunch settled in for the night, at least the children. Going to bed with the sun going down was the way things were done on our trip west. We rose with the sun and worked hard all day. By the time the evening sunset, we were ready to turn in. Mary and I stepped into the brush, out of the firelight to relieve ourselves. Chase was aware and alert but knew we would not go far.

Once we returned to firelight, Mary excused herself and went off to join Ned and her children, who were retiring to bed.

One of the Parker children was sharing the back of my wagon to sleep in. It was warmer and more protective of little four-year-old

Tom. He took up hardly any room and was comforted by being in the back of the wagon. I liked it too.

Chase and I didn't want to say good night but knew we would have an early and long day tomorrow. He walked me to the back of the wagon and touched my hand to his cheek before assisting me up. Chase banked the fire and went to his wagon.

Chapter Twenty-Three

THE MORNING WAS DIM white with a crusty light frost on all the exposed surfaces. Oxen and horses were not exempt. Coffee pots were already on fires that had been fed some dry wood by early risers. I added a pot of water for tea drinkers. The warmth would feel good. Most everyone was rubbing their hands together or slapping their shoulders trying to get the blood to flowing.

Little Tom crawled out of the wagon with a sleepy look as he snuggled up next to me. He whispered that he needed to use the privy right away. I took his little hand and led him away for some privacy. After Tom and I had taken some privacy, he asked if I could help him get his coat on. He had managed to get his boots on but they needed to be tied, which I accommodated. When we got back to the wagon we quickly got his coat on him and delivered him into his mother's morning arms, something that they both needed.

Breakfast was really more of an energy break with only coffee or tea and berries and pine nuts to munch on. The children at our fires also got a half of a boiled egg. Mary Robertson had been gifted six eggs. She said the children would get them and that meant all the children in our five-rig camp. There were 10 children. There was simply no way she would give them to her own children as the others looked on. So they each got half.

Mary was watching her children become more angular each day. The Robertson children and the adults were doing the same. I have never witnessed a more reasonable group of people in my life. They shared and assisted before even being asked. That was not to say that they didn't get angry because everyone's temper was getting sharper, but they made an effort to think before acting. And for that, I applauded them.

Chase had finished outfitting his team and came over to my wagon to assist me. He mentioned he should be quicker since Mister Gill and Adam Parker both showed up about the same time. I had fed my team and made sure that their water bucket was not covered in ice so they were hydrated. They were obviously cold. Between the four of us, we had my team ready to roll in a matter of minutes.

Tonight, I was pulling a couple of horse blankets out from under kitchenware and putting them on my oxen. Brad also mentioned to us this morning that he had some oats that he would be sharing tonight. Hopefully, it would keep our animals motivated to step up. He brought extra in his wagon but did not want to use it when feed was still ample among us. Now, with the colder temperatures and less food, the animals needed it.

As everyone was taking care of morning details, we heard a commotion at both ends of the train. We were not sure if it was Indians or another gravesite. But we quickly found out what it was. The men had checked their traps, and they were both occupied! Dennis had trapped a large fox and Rush, who was doing most of the clamor, had trapped a squirrel. *My goodness, what will happen when he traps a larger animal?* But, in all fairness, we were excited and know that it meant a couple of pots tonight would have a little extra seasoning. It put a smile on everyone's face as they started the day. Rush couldn't stop smiling as he delivered the squirrel to Mrs. Brahm for tonight's stewpot. *He is feeling pretty good about his contribution, as he should.*

Before leaving, I gathered a handful of dry beans from Mary and from Mrs. Robertson to add to what I had, and put a pot of beans on to soak. They wouldn't be ready tonight, but they would be ready when we had our day layover. We were all looking forward to that day because it was something different. I couldn't say it was a day of rest, because it wouldn't be. But the trail wrung people out dry from the day in and day out of the drudgery. It only got worse as the weather got colder. We had less food, and the time remaining to reach our home got shorter. *Yes, I think we will all enjoy our day of work, hot food, and fellowship.*

Brad called for us to "load up." Dennis loped ahead with his long rifle in one hand and his trap in the other. He let us know that he was going ahead to place his trap in the hope that we will have more meat at the campfire tonight, possibly even a deer. He also mentioned to the young girls that they might want to have a container handy as they walk, since we were in Huckleberry Country. Now, I had no idea what Huckleberry Country was and neither did the girls. He told them, "Huckleberries grow heavily in the western territories. They are about as big as the end of your little finger, dark blue, almost black, and very juicy. They also stain everything they touch so don't get them on your clothes unless you plan on living with that color. They are great for pies but you have to pick a lot of them because they are so small."

Sounds like the next couple of days could be a learning experience for all of us, or at least most of us.

The ground was a little uneven but there was not as much rock as in the days before. It was more uneven ground because of ruts from the trees and other natural debris that had "clogged up" the natural trail. If there was such a thing as a natural trail. Titus Ross and Adam Parker made it their jobs to march in front of the lead wagon with the machete, clearing anything that stood in our way, or redirecting Mister Gill, the lead, around it. They kept us moving. We made good time today, stopping late afternoon for the day with only a brief stop in the afternoon for everyone to catch their breath, use the bushes for some private time, and to allow for a few of the younger ones who were not riding to catch up.

Once we stopped activity started. Camps were set up. It seemed we were smack dab in the middle of Huckleberry Country, as Dennis had alerted us, so the girls immediately started gathering berries. The little ones gathered sticks for starting our fires. My pot of beans that I had put on to soak was brought out and put over our fire. Dennis had skinned out the fox, and Mary Parker had it basting in some type of sauce after cutting it into small pieces for a stew, rolling the pieces in acorn flour, and salting it. She had already put water, wild onions, and mushrooms into the pot and now added the fox meat. I found my mouth watering just thinking about the stew.

Chase appeared to amble towards me but I knew that he was actually keeping me foremost in his mind. I was taking the gear off my oxen and getting them comfortable for the night. He took over, and I was glad for his assistance. I couldn't imagine how the weight of the yolk and all the lines and hookups felt to the animals. I was doing my best to pay attention to their needs.

Thank goodness Pa and Nalan both taught me to always take care of your animals first. They could be the difference between you making it or not. Even though I knew how to take care of them, it would be easy to overlook something at the end of each day, being as we were so tired. *I'm thankful I have strong arms to help me.*

Brad came by and asked Chase if he would come with him and collect a few buckets from others so that he could get the oats distributed to everyone as he had promised. Mister Gill was with him as well, and he was bringing two buckets. They filled their buckets and started down the row with Mister Gill headed toward the front of the train, with Chase starting in the middle and working his way towards Mister Gill, and Brad starting in the middle and working his way backwards. Once finished, he asked Solomon to start checking on brakes before dark. Brad would join him after getting the oats in the hands of our teamsters.

Solomon and Brad went to the front of the train and moved back. They were pleasantly surprised that most of the wagons were looking pretty good. The heaviest wagons, the Conestogas, showed most of the wear, which made total sense. Those Conestogas that needed it would get new brakes tonight before going downhill tomorrow morning. The wheels would wait until tomorrow.

These wagons could carry more weight than the other wagons because of their size. Many of them were 48 inches wide, 18 feet long (including the tongue) and 11 feet high. They were designed for moving freight. The ones on our train were not that big and were not being pulled by as large a team. Nor did they carry the full weight. Oxen were not like horses. I'd never seen one speed up or try to run like horses did. Indians weren't interested in stealing them; they wanted horses. So it made them a better bet that you'd get to the end of the trail with your team intact (although there were never any guarantees).

Wheel work would be done on flat ground tomorrow, unless there was something that wouldn't make it down the hill safely. It appeared that Brad and Solomon were in agreement that all wagons were worthy of making it down the hill, and they would be doing the needed maintenance at that time.

It was good tonight in our camps. Dennis came in carrying another fox, which he took to the Braham's camp cook pot. He left it up to them to share however they saw fit. Of course, Mrs. Brahm asked Tanner Wiggins to skin and prepare it for their stewpot. Tanner was prompt with the request, and it was simmering in no time. Mrs. Brahm asked the other camps around her to add something to the pot if they would like to supp together. Everyone was happy to do that and to join in for supper.

The girls had come in with a full bucket of huckleberries, picked fresh. They decided to keep them until tomorrow at "the flats"— what I decided to call our level-ground location. We would be rearranging wagons, working on them, and having a big communal supper with everyone there.

It would be the perfect time to make huckleberry pies or cobblers. We could, between all of us, rustle up all the ingredients and have ourselves a real feast.

Brad would give the lineup for two days forward, the start-up time for tomorrow, and any special instructions.

I'm so excited. This will be a great opportunity to meet everyone and maybe there will be music, and maybe, just maybe, there will be dancing with Chase.

We gathered more wood for the fires and covered it to keep it dry for a quick-start fire in the morning. Everyone was looking forward to tomorrow, almost as if it were a festival. I supposed it was. It had been months with just each other for company. It would help to expand our friendships to others on the train besides those friends we made in the wagons closest to our own.

I tried to watch what was happening around me and did pretty well most of the time. But I was missing what happened with the middle travelers in our train. I heard tell that the folks there had smaller families, and most of them came from Missouri rather than Fort Hall. I was looking forward to meeting all of them, especially the womenfolk. *Do any of them have any books with them?*

After supper was pretty much done, each wagon sent one person to represent their rig. We met at the fifth wagon camp, which happened to be mine. Mary Parker had already taken little Tom to do his private business and say goodnight to his family. He gave his Pa a hug as he carried him back to my wagon and tucked him in. I could tell it was a treat for both of them.

Brad let folks chat a little before calling things to order. He said we would do our usual morning routine and then start down the hill. The difference would be that those walking would go first. All of them, with Dennis and Mrs. Gill walking out, away from the descending wagons. He wanted drivers only in the seat of wagon, no one else riding, especially children. Even though the slope was not considered as treacherous as others we had already descended, and would go down eventually, he wanted no chance of a wagon slamming into a tree, or worse, one of our family members. We were to keep at least three wagon-lengths in-between as we descended.

Titus had offered to drive my wagon down the hill, but I had chosen to take my wagon down this mountain myself. Even though I appreciated the offer, and I made sure I communicated that, I needed to show myself that I could be responsible for my own wagon. Which, of course, did not mean that I did not appreciate occasional help and support. I was sure there would be times in the future that I would be more than ready to accept that same proposal.

Mister Linde said he was sure that while going down the hill, Mrs. Linde would be happy to give over the reins to Tanner. He went on to say that Mrs. Linde was not all that comfortable going down hills or crossing rivers. It was agreed that Tanner would take the wagon down the hill to the next overnight location.

According to Brad, it was going to be a short day if all went well. He told us we would be camping close to the river. He said the crossing place was called Tailholt. He mentioned that animals would be drinking from the same river, hopefully not at the same location, and so would Indians. No need to be scared at this point, but certainly we needed to be aware and prepared. He wasn't sure what all, if anything, was there. What he could tell us was that we would change the wagon position lineup when we left the flats.

Tomorrow would also be a workday. How hard it would become depended largely on how many wagons needed maintenance. He wanted all wagon owners to help, especially when it came to lifting wagons so that the wheels could be soaked. He asked that those who had good, strong, young men bring them along, except for Titus.

Brad warned us that we needed to be aware that there could be Indians or wild animals that we were unaware of, so everyone needed to use caution. He asked Titus, Rocky, and Ben to scout around close to our travelers to keep them safe. Dennis would expand the territory he scouted, as well as look for possible places where we could cross the river.

We were all told to allow ourselves some time tomorrow night to get to know others and commune with them. Let the womenfolk know that it would be a great time to pull out the recipes that they have the ingredients for and get ready to shake the dust off.

The big news that we had all been waiting for was the new lineup to start day after tomorrow when we left "the flats." It went as follows:

1. Mister & Mrs. Gill — 2 Married man & wife
2. Ross Family — 1 nephew + Mister & Mrs.
3. Mrs. Linde — 2 Married woman & husband
4. Rush Spencer — 1 Single Man
5. Brahm Family — 5 children + 2 parents
6. Solomon Whittacker — 1 Single Man
7. Chase Gunner — 1 Single Man
8. Robertson Family — 8 children + Joseph & Anna
9. Questa — 1 Widow
10. Parker Family — 5 children + Ned & Mary Parker
11. McCall Family — 2 children + Jack & Delia McCall
12. Wiggins Family — 2 children + Mister Wiggins
13. Base Family — 4 children + Nathan & Harriet Base
14. Issac True — 3 children + Issac & Olive
15. Wesley Collard — 1 child, expect 2nd + Wesley & Cora
16. Horace Close — 2 Newly married, Horace & Minnie
17. James Sickler — 3 children + James & Mahala
18. Amos Gode — 1 child (Calvin)+ single man

19. George Baker   3 children + George & Hannah

20. Daniel Dawson   2 married Daniel & Josephine

Adding Brad, Rocky, and Ben, and that put us over 80 that we had counted.

Brad wasn't through. He surprised me, all of us, probably. Before breaking up the meeting, he reminded us that everyone in the camp needed to pull their load. To chip in when needed, without being asked. He said that our women, especially, were under very heavy loads with managing children, childbirth, cooking, and doing laundry, in addition helping with the animals.

He shared that many of the womenfolk were already on the trip westward against their wishes. They were there simply to appease their husbands who were following their own dream.

"Don't give your women, your partner, extra fodder to make the trip harder than it already is," he told the men. "Talk to your older children and make sure they have a chore to finish each day. It should not only be helping, but taking a load off their Mom and you whenever it is possible. Make going west a family dream."

Brad continued: "It's a good way to prepare for tomorrow and whatever the rest of the trip brings us. What it boils down to is that we will be more successful in reaching our destination if everyone does their share. And everyone will be much happier once you get there, wherever THAT is."

After everyone stepped away, Chase asked if I had time to talk for a bit. I made time. Chase and I sat by the fire and discussed what was said at the meeting. "Is what Brad said about women going west to appease their husbands true?" he asked.

"It had been that way with me," I said. "My husband had never asked me what I wanted. He made the plans and announced that's what we were doing. He married me so he could check 'wife' off his list: wife-check. I did not want to leave my family and everything I knew, but he was my husband and I obeyed. It was too late for me to turn around when I found myself out on the desert with my husband's dead body and no one to turn to."

Chase was quiet for some time before he took my hand in his large calloused hand and said, "Questa, you are one heck of a woman. I know we are not married or even promised to each other yet. But I promise you, I'm going to do everything in my power to help make things go smoother for you. I can't promise it will be good, but hopefully it will be better than it would be without me." He went on to say that he wanted to show me what kind of man he was by his actions before he came to me with serious questions and that he wanted to protect me.

I looked at Chase with what might have been considered tears by some. To others they were definitely stars in my eyes.

"Chase, you have already been helping me and smoothing the way for me. You've been wonderful. I will try to help you as well. We will get through this together."

He kissed my forehead, said goodnight, and walked off to his wagon like the gentleman he was.

Chapter Twenty-Four

As stated by Brad the evening before, the morning routine was pretty much the same as it had been, except that the animals were treated to grain in addition to their usual hay. The grain would energize them a little and warm them up enough to be interested in moving in the cold, very brisk air. I had put some horse blankets over them last night to help. At least it kept the frost off their lean bodies.

Dennis came in with a possum from his catch this morning. He had already skinned it out. It went to the Robertson stewpot, which didn't really matter tonight since we were all sharing in a communal meal, anyway.

Mrs. Linde, Dennis, the children, and the Mrs. from each wagon, except for me, started down the mountain on foot. Titus followed with his loaded gun, continually fanning back and forth on the flank. Rocky and Ben were on horseback in front and to the sides of the walkers. Dennis walked in front, carrying the machete in case it was needed to clear obstacles. Titus brought up the flank, and Rocky and Ben covered the sides. The women and children were surrounded. In addition, Martin Linde led a couple of saddle horses that had been tied behind wagons. Cordelia Base, 19, was next to Delia McCall, who was leading their milk cows and the two younger McCall girls.

If any Indians were around, this would be a true test. Stealing milk cows and horses, and possibly womenfolk and children, would possibly be a big coup, depending on the personality of this tribe of rogues. If it were going to happen, it was also an opportune time for the Indians to attack the wagons. No extra firepower there with all the men managing their wagons down a decline. That was another item for our prayer list.

The first part of the group was down the hill and out of sight before Jesse Gill tapped his lead oxen on the backside and said, "Step up!" in a firm and commanding tone. Down the hill, bumping and creaking, he slowly crawled with his team, following Brad's lead. Jesse made sure that his oxen were even as they moved down the incline, keeping his hand on his brake handle while applying mild pressure as needed.

As he moved along, Brad gave the sign to the Ross wagon to start moving. Elijah Ross was probably a bit more cautious than normal. I thought that had a lot to do with the fact that he and Linde lost animals and a wagon a couple of months back. It was because they weren't listening to Brad. Well, he was listening now. Third in line on Evelyn Linde's behalf, Tanner motioned to his single ox to "step up" as he took him slowly down with an amount of patience that most grown men did not exhibit. These young men and women grew up fast in the west, and even faster while they were fighting their way there.

The wagons continued to travel downhill, one by one, reaching flat ground, rejoicing, and moving along to catch up to those on foot, level out their rigs, and start setting up for the remainder of their big day. The wagons in front traveled for a good 30 minutes before meeting up with those walking ahead. As they arrived, they attempted to circle the wagons as best as they could. They left room to work on the wagons and to set up campfires for communal meals and conversation tonight.

Everyone helped, from the youngest to the oldest. Taking care of the animals was the first priority. A highline was strung close by with natural barriers of berry vines on one side so horses and oxen would not wander off. The troughs and the tubs for linseed oil were removed from those wagons that had them. Cook pots were unloaded and set on slow fires with ample water to avoid burning. Others added to the pots according to what they had. There were at least six pots stewing with squirrel, possum, or some other type of wild critter that didn't get away. As always, pots of coffee were available at each campfire as well. It would have warded off the cold, but for now, everyone was so busy that the movement was enough to warm them.

The first wagon wheels that would need soaking in linseed oil were the three Conestogas. Because of their size and added weight, all menfolk were asked to rally. Before picking up the wagons to place the wheels in the troughs, dirty laundry, and water buckets were handed out of the wagons to the womenfolk. There would be no climbing in the wagon while it was blocked up. For safety reasons, as well as for any additional weight.

They soaked two wheels at a time in the linseed. The linseed covered about one-third of the wheel. They turned them at two-hour intervals. This went on all day while other activities took place. Amos Gode's wagon, carrying extra supplies for Brad, and Mrs. Linde's buckboard, had both been done the night before. Because they were lighter wagons, they were able to manage picking the wagon up and soaking all four wheels at one time by using other troughs and tubs.

Solomon was checking brakes as the day wore on. He ended up assisting brake replacement on Brahm's Conestoga. Jozeph had planned ahead and brought extra brake pads. Together he and Solomon made quick and expert work of applying the new pad. They also checked the brake lever to make sure there were no cracks or other surprises. The condition was good. Solomon could see that Mister Brahm had taken good care of his wagon. But with five children, the man looked tired. Of course, not nearly as tired as his wife Marsha looked—she was expecting another child. She was not sure on the exact date, because she said she had been so busy keeping track of the others that the date had gotten by her.

Marsha had walked up that hill a couple of days ago, leading children from five- to 14 years old. Her three older children, 14, 12, and 11, were old enough to help with the younger two at five and nine years old. That was, of course, as long as the older ones weren't in any need. It still fell on Marsha to cook and wash laundry— although her Rachael and Betsy were very helpful with that—help with the rig, and keep her husband Jozeph aimed in the direction of his dream of moving westward.

Marsha instructed 14-year-old Elisha to assist his Dad, but to first pull out the tarps that they would use tonight to sleep under and to do it before the wagon went for wheel repairs. Elisha dreamed of being a grown-up man, and was very happy to assist. Especially when it was what he considered "a man's job" that he was completing.

Dennis and Titus had led everyone, in groups, to the river and back, some 100 yards away from the camp. They were staying close to the womenfolk with their loaded guns, yet allowing them some private time.

The river was available for man and beast. Therefore, knowing that and preparing for it was very important. Whenever anyone went down, there were always at least two menfolk with loaded guns and eagle eyes.

After arriving, the horses were led to the river to drink their fill. The oxen would be watered by bucket in camp. The women searched out several large flat rocks with relatively clean water flowing through. They would use the rocks to pound out the stains and the thickness of dust and dirt that settled in since they were last able to do laundry.

Chase and I worked closely and quietly together, completing our chores for the two teams of oxen and setting up our campfires with coffee pot and bean pot, leaving the lid on so the water wouldn't boil away. I asked Chase for his laundry as I loaded up a basket of my own to take to the river. He was getting ready to help the menfolk with the soaking of the wagon wheels.

He gave me such a look of surprise and said, "You don't have to do that, Questa."

I smiled and said, "You're doing the hardest part of carrying the load to the river, and don't forget, I expect you to carry it back, too. I don't expect to keep score, Chase Gunner. You do for me. Now get your items for me; we're wasting precious daylight."

Chase walked me to the river, along with Titus with his gun, and a couple of other ladies who had laundry ready to go. Once he placed the laundry next to the rock, he backed up, smiled, tipped his hat, and walked back to the camp and his duties.

Dennis, along with Titus, was back and forth, watching over all of us. But they were also checking traps. Dennis told Titus that he would need to do the watching over for a little bit. He had caught the trail of a nice-sized deer, and he was going to follow it. Titus rose to the challenge and kept us bundled closer.

Most folks on the trail only had two sets of clothes, if they were lucky. They were wearing a set that could also use some cleaning. The best way to clean those clothes was to go into the water with their soap and bathe while clothed. In the summer months, that may not have been a problem, but it was not the summer months. It was very cold. Just putting my legs in the water numbed them.

Our first set of clothes was hanging over branches and tree limbs. I made a choice to take my underclothes off and wash them, as did some of the others. We were hoping they would be dry by tonight; otherwise, we would be setting a new trend!

Dennis was gone no more than two hours when he showed up headed back to camp with a deer on his shoulders. He had out-smarted it. That meant tonight we would not only have food, but we would have venison and other tasty choices. *I think we can stop worrying about having enough food for the next several days. Even though we are nigh 100 people, give or take, in this company.*

Dennis had other news as well. He said that during his scout-ing he found bear scat. From that he could tell that they've been on their "fall diet," eating berries and such. They were getting ready to rest for the winter, which meant they needed to eat something sustainable for the winter months when they hibernated. The bear had also been scouting his river territory. Everything needed water, which made the access to the river very attractive. He said chances were that it was a brown or a black bear, but he may have had the attitude of a grizzly. Either way, we would not win in a face-to-face showdown with any type of bear. We needed a plan.

Dennis said that the deer would be hung outside the camp, off the ground in a tree, until it was prepared for eating. The carcass would be moved further away from camp and left for other varmints to clean up. Normally he would tan the hide himself, but not with the bear so close to camp. As soon as possible, the venison would need to be cut up, and cooked or cured so as not to attract the bear to our camps.

Within minutes, Chase and several of the husbands showed up with strong arms to lend us a hand. They gave us time to gather our freshly washed laundry off the branches and put it in our baskets. Because Chase also carried a loaded rifle, and we had taken Dennis very seriously, he carried his rifle in his right hand and held onto one side of the basket. I held the other, and we walked back to camp. I noticed the others were doing the same thing.

Because the air was damp and cold, I pulled my tarp out and strung it from the side of my wagon to the Robertson wagon, leaving Anna and me to share a clothesline that Jesse and Joseph rigged up for us. I didn't need much room for my freshly washed clothing. Anna, however, had lots for us to hang up for her big family.

Titus made a sweep of the riverbank to make sure no one or no clothing item had been left behind. When he returned to camp, he had a smile covering his face and was holding a big fish by the tail. It was one that was caught in our water trap.

This land is so rich. It has berries and water and lots of animals to keep us fed. I'm beginning to believe the stories could be true. Maybe fish really do jump six feet out of the water, and deer run through our yards. Water is clean and abundant in this territory of Oregon. I'm so excited about reaching "Eden," this land of plenty. For now, the sun still shines, and we're a little chilly from our hands and feet being submerged in the cold river water.

Once back in camp, we discovered that some of the young men had followed suit and strung clothesline from the bows of each wagon to a tree or another wagon for the damp clothes to hang. They kept in mind that work was still going on with many of the wagons.

Camp was very busy, but organized. It looked like a small city with everyone taking care of their duties and chipping in to help others. Folks were stopping and saying a few words to others in passing. They were meeting new folks and figuring out who they would be traveling with tomorrow, or the next day, when they left the "flats."

I'm a people watcher, especially on this trip where I have so many to watch. At home on the farm, there wasn't much activity. But here, especially today, it was teeming with activity and hope and excitement. As I was watching, Solomon Whittacker stopped and turned around when Cordelia Base passed him. He literally stopped in his tracks. He looked as if he had been struck dumb. Cordelia, on the other hand, made it just past three wagons before she stopped and turned to face Solomon. After a silence that was deafening, they both broke out in bright smiles and walked toward each other.

Cordelia was carrying a few of her laundry items to hang. Without a word, Solomon took the basket from her hands. Ever-so-softly, he introduced himself. She, in turn, did the same. He asked her which wagon was hers and could he walk her there. She assented, and as if propelled, they turned and slowly walked in the direction of her wagon. Neither wanted to give up a second spent with each other.

They looked lovely together. Solomon's tall, broad shoulders and thick, wavy, chocolate brown hair were a compliment to Cordelia's waist-length golden tresses and statuesque frame. She was as outspoken as he was quiet. Both were very respectful to others.

Solomon asked her if she would dance with him tonight if there was music. She said that she would be waiting for tonight with anticipation of seeing him again. At that point, Solomon asked Cordelia if he could meet her mother and father, Harriet and Nathan. She said yes, but it would have to be tonight, since they were both elsewhere at the moment. In the meantime, she told him that Brad had asked her and Kate Wiggins to take an inventory of food stores in each wagon. She also needed to get back to her younger siblings and keep an eye on them. She explained that she had three younger siblings: Leta was 14, Joel 10, and Jasper eight years old. She said that Leta was a big help, but since this was a workday, they were doing double duty to help their Ma. Solomon told her he understood and would see her tonight.

Solomon returned to the wagons that needed wheels to be switched or reinstalled. Cordelia went to the next wagon, after hanging her laundry out of the way as best she could.

Kate and Cordelia, although five years difference in age, were becoming fast friends. It was probably because they were both well-educated and enjoyed good, thought-provoking conversations. I thought it would be perfect if Kate would get Cordelia to work with her on the school that started late afternoon today at the Wiggins site. With so many things happening, it would be a very short class today. The plan was to use it mostly to figure out the level of abilities for each of the students.

The two young women found some writing implements and journals and started out to do their job checking food stores as requested by Brad. They found that a number of folks were not in their wagons due to the other work that was going on in camp. If folks were near their wagon, they could not get in them because of the work being done. They talked it over and decided they would suggest to Brad that a discussion be had before dinner tonight with everyone there. To the best of their abilities, each person could tell them what they had left. In the meantime, they needed to prepare for the first day of school.

Little did we know that another important discussion was already taking place with Dennis, Brad, and whoever else happened to be close by listening or participating in the discussion. They were talking bear seriously. Dennis said he had not only brought a deer right through our camp, but also a fish. Both were what the bear might consider his dinner. He would be coming to claim it.

"There's no way to protect everyone and our foodstuffs from the bear every minute," Dennis said. "As it gets colder and the bear prepares for the first snow of winter, he becomes more aggressive."

More discussion ensued before Brad laid it out to Dennis and asked him what he suggested. Dennis said simply, "If we had a bear trap, that would be helpful."

Amos Gode immediately responded that he was carrying a bear trap on his wagon. Even though it wasn't a required piece of equipment, he'd decided to throw it in. At this point, Amos was looking pretty popular. Dennis asked him to get it and meet him at the beginning of the trail to the river. He asked Titus to go get the fish that they caught earlier and bring it to the same place, along with his loaded rifle.

The men met at the beginning of the trail. Dennis asked them to follow him and to try not to touch anything other than what they carried. They went 150 feet downriver from where we had been watering and doing laundry. It was a brushy area with good animal access and scat from the bear. Dennis set the bear trap with its mighty jaws locked open and used the fish as bait. He broke a branch and swished it around the ground and threw it over the trap haphazardly, being careful not to set it off. They all pretty much backed out of the trail, dusting it as they went with sticks and brush.

They all went back to camp, but in a more roundabout way so as to avoid coming straight to camp.

Dennis and Brad reiterated that no one was to go out alone or out of sight of an overseer with a ready rifle.

The rest of the men were still changing out wagon wheels as soaking was completed. Children had been gathering firewood or berries in sight of camp. They were instructed to collect as much dry firewood as possible in order to avoid creating any more smoke than necessary. The young ones were showing up at their wagons for a scrubbing and readiness for their "first day" of school. There was an excitement in the air for the children as well as for Kate. Cordelia had agreed to help and was standing by.

Thirteen children showed up at the Wiggins wagon and class began as a paper was passed around for them to write their names, first and last, followed by their age. *That is, if they can write. If they can't, their signature will be absent.* A circle of stumps, logs, and boxes had been pulled around to resemble a classroom, or at least to create places for the students to sit.

Of the 13 children, about half could write their name, either first or last or both. Those same children could write their age number. The rest were a mixed bag of ages and awareness. A couple of the children were only five years old, so had not yet started school. Still, they should be able to write their first name and at least know their last name.

Kate and Cordelia had decided that once they got familiar with the students by name, they would ignore their ages, and have an open conversation in the hope of finding out what aspirations they had to learn to read and to write. Was it because their parents required it or for another reason?

The young instructors explained that they would like for any books, paper, or pencils each student had to be brought to class tomorrow and each night they attend class. They also explained that it was very important that they not miss school once they've started. What they would be learning would build on the prior day's instruction. Kate said without something to practice on, it would be hard to look at their letters and numbers and practice them.

A small area of dirt that was clear of brush was used to show the first lesson and possibly the first homework assignment. Cordelia wrote each student's name in the dirt as they spoke. She also wrote their age immediately after their name. Kate showed each student how their name and their age looked as it was printed on the dirt slate. They left the writing on the ground for the students to pass by and look at, then to attempt to copy. The class was short, less than an hour.

The camp was busier than a honeybee collecting honey. Everyone was wrapping up their chores, completing the task of maintenance on the wagons, doing laundry, harvesting berries and herbs along the trail, and making sure those simmering pots of precious meat, with acorn flour to thicken the contents and fresh picked herbs, were cooking at the right speed and not burning.

Brad asked the menfolk who could shoot and carry rifles to set up a schedule for camp. He wanted two men for a one-hour shift starting immediately. "Circle the camp on alert for any intruders," Brad said. "That means not only Indians, but also animals." Dennis and Titus said they would take the first shift as they walked out to the edge of the gathered wagons.

Folks started to assemble around the cook pots, some bringing biscuits or some other contribution to the special evening. As they showed, many had taken a turn at their washing facilities. That turn consisted mostly of washing their face, neck, and remaining body parts with a wet, cold rag dipped in the river. The weather was downright cold and the river even colder.

Chapter Twenty-Five

Most of the women had made sure that they and their children shook as much dirt off as possible, in addition to receiving a shining up. Because the weather had been so cold, our freshly-washed laundry was not dry. In fact, it was stiff and damp. One thing we all did besides dusting ourselves off was to make sure our hair was combed and managed well, and we removed our bonnets and hats. After all, it was a social that most of us had experienced sometime in our lives. Although it was probably a fancier affair than those of the past. For us, it simply couldn't have been more exciting.

Chase showed up looking mighty handsome. I could tell he was tired, as we all were. But he brought his gentlemanly concern for me, as well as his appetite. He had scrubbed the dirt off and done his best to remove the linseed oil and any grease that might have covered his hands. As uncomfortable as it must have been, he had shaved his handsome face with a straight razor and cold water. I am pretty sure that was done on my behalf.

Before Titus walked off to do his first hour of guard duty, he asked me to please let Betha Robertson know that he would be back soon and was looking forward to dinner and dancing with her.

Dennis made it clear to Titus before they set out on their duties that he would have to be alert. There would be lots of commotion around the camp, and it might be hard for him to hear clearly or stop harm before it started. Based on the serious look on Titus' face and on the way he had treated every responsibility so far, I had total faith in him.

When Betha showed up, I passed the message along from Titus. She wore an ecstatic smile. I could see that Betha had taken extra care in her appearance. I knew she would, being the sweet and caring young woman that she was. She was such a pretty girl with her blond hair and sparkling blue eyes, which were brighter than any sky. She radiated youth, even with the trail marking her. Among her personal belongings, she had managed to keep her blue hair ribbon clean, and now had it tied nicely to show off her soft blonde curls. It was apparent that she had saved it for just such an occasion. She had also dabbed a smidge of some type of oil on her lips to take away the dryness. *I'm sure Titus will be very taken with her and appreciative of her efforts to look extra special.*

I applauded everyone's efforts to clean up, being tired and all. I noticed that everyone took the time to be presentable, even though they all were wearing their heaviest coats and wraps to ward off the cold. They were making it very clear that they would not allow their spirits to be cold and damp as well.

The smells of the camp made us salivate. The pots had variations of vegetables, thickener, and meat in them. All were hot, full of satisfying ingredients, and there was enough for everyone to eat their fill. That had not been the norm for more than a couple of weeks now. Stewpots bubbled, and the smell of huckleberry cobbler scented the entire camp. It took a lot of huckleberries to make a cobbler, but it was certainly appreciated when we tasted it. Those who liked it most—which was obvious by the blue stains on their tongues and lips—faced considerable teasing.

Brad called our attention to a couple of important messages after folks had a chance at some supper. His big reminder and message was that of the care that must be taken every day. Especially when we were camped next to access to a water source. He was very specific about bears, cougars, badgers, and, of course, Indians.

I especially felt the unease of the bear warning, since I had already had a very close encounter. Brad let everyone know that we would have guards changing every hour throughout the night. He reiterated that even if you weren't on duty, you needed to be aware: "For everyone doing personal business, make someone aware, with a gun, who would protect you from intruders." He informed us that bear scat had been found downriver about 150 feet, and a trap had been set for the bear.

"It may or may not get in the trap," he said, "and the trap may or may not hold it. Be aware. The same applies to our access to water. Badgers and cougars are abundant in this brushy part of the country. They blend in well and are hard to spot."

We had been warned against Indians in the past. We'd been lucky and hoped that our luck would hold. In the meantime, we got it: *be aware!*

Kate and Cordelia were the next to speak. They asked if each wagon could give them a verbal inventory of how much food they had left, and what type of food it was. We would be passing some territory ahead where it would be hard to harvest because of rocky canyons and mountains. More discussion would follow after the inventory was done in a couple of days.

School was discussed with a reminder that each day after camp was set up, school would start within 30 to 60 minutes, depending on the weather and the natural light. They also reminded their students to bring any writing implements, paper, journals, or slates that they had, and to not miss any classes because one lesson was built on the one before it.

Brad gave one last note and reiterated our lineup for our departure. "There's a good chance that we'll leave tomorrow at midday," he said, "or even the day after, because of the preparation for the crossing. I'll be letting everyone know tomorrow or later tonight."

Then the music started. Fiddles, banjos, a guitar or two, and even castanets showed up. There were several washboards and spoons pulled from the back of wagons. The men, and a few of the women, sung, took turns playing with the evolving band, and dancing with their mates or children. They played songs like "Molly Bawn" and "De Boatman's Dance" and some songs I had never heard. I didn't see a tired one in the bunch. A feeling of camaraderie like no other prevailed.

Chase was quick to ask for the first dance. His big smile and large, hard-baked hands touched me with nothing but care and affection. He wasn't hiding his feelings and neither was I.

I had brushed my thick hair tonight until it had shone its brightest and made sure that I had used some of the soothing aloe lotion from my small plant on my hands and face, and especially on my lips. I'd shaken out my dress well and had a coat over the top of it, which would soon be removed. I was warming up quickly. Although I wasn't sure if it was from the exercise of dancing or because Chase was holding me and looking at me like no one else existed. It was a good thing he didn't have guard duty until the next round. I was pretty sure he would not see or hear anything like a bear or an Indian. His mind and eyes were definitely on me, and I definitely liked it.

We danced about four dances before he had to take his turn as guard. In the meantime, I could use the rest and take time to meet some of the other folks.

Titus had come back and went right to Betha. They were making eyes at each other, and trying to talk, but not having much luck with that. The music and the laughing were too loud. Both began to diminish as people danced more. Throughout the evening, I saw lots of the young folks including Emily Robertson and Adam Parker, Will Robertson and Trish Parker, Solomon Whittacker and Cordelia Base, just to name a few. Lots of friendships and romances were sprouting up, especially since we'd had a chance to get to know folks better. Changing the lineup would encourage more of that again.

The married couples were doing quite a lot of dancing and socializing as well. Of course, they had to trade off to watch their young ones, so that the men could take guard duty. I, for certain, recognized Joseph and Anna Robertson, the Gills, Delia and Jack McCall, Wesley and Cora Collard, Jozeph and Marsha Brahm, who were managing the slower dances with rest in between due to Marsha being "in the family way." Ned and Mary Parker were there. It did my heart good to see them having some fun.

The smaller children were jumping around in groups, as young ones would do. Parents paid special attention to them to be sure they stayed away from the fires and did not touch any of the loaded rifles that sat around the camp. Children were taught at an early age to never pick up a firearm unless you were taught to and had a reason to kill something. Guns were not toys.

Titus had long since completed his guard duty and was not missing a moment with Betha. They moved to the outside of the circle to seat themselves on a log away from the music. They looked at each other and talked quietly, forgetting that anyone else existed.

When Chase returned, we had one more dance, and then we also took to the outside circle for conversation. "Did you have an opportunity to meet Solomon Whittacker or Edmond Wiggins?" he asked about these single men. He watched my face carefully as he asked. He waited for my response only briefly before asking, "Did you have an opportunity to meet—"

I touched his lips with my fingers gently to shush him.

"I have been introduced to Solomon Whittacker by his interest, Cordelia," I said. "He seemed nice enough, and Cordelia says he's sweeter than sugar. I also had met Edmond, who likes to be called Ed, briefly during our camp meeting tonight. He seemed grateful to be here and still has excitement about his westward move. He's really thankful that his two nearly-grown children are finding friends, and that they are involved with the members of the company."

Then I said, "Since the Parkers and the Robertsons are in front and back of me for the lineup, that left Whittacker and Wiggins for me to get to know."

Chase seemed a bit more relaxed with my explanation.

The music started to wind down as the folks gathered their eating utensils and bowls to be washed. They didn't have to scrape the bowls much at all, but they did before putting them into a pot of hot water to clean. Several folks helped to put things back to rights, including taking their eating sets to their wagons with them; they made quick work of it. Mothers and fathers were making sure their children had done the private business before getting them tucked in for the night. It had never warmed up today, although the dancing and holding hands helped for a bit. Tarps had already been fitted over bedrolls next to wagons. Some laundry was still hung under wagons so they didn't drip or gather more moisture from the cold night air.

My oxen may have looked like they were special because I had put their "coats" (horse blankets) on their boney backs again tonight, after petting them and calling them sweet names.

Chase continued to help me with my chores, especially hitching and unhitching my oxen, morning and evening. We pretty much had a routine, and yet we didn't take each other for granted. Tonight, as he held my hand, he told me:

"I've come to care a great deal for you, and I look forward to every day, even the very hard ones, with hills to climb and little food and rest, because I know that I'm going to see your beautiful, sweet smile and gorgeous hair, and hear your easy laugh."

I couldn't stop myself from telling Chase:

"I care for you. Actually, it's more than care. I, too, look forward to each coming day."

At that point, we both knew we were promised to each other. He hugged me; I stood on my tiptoes and kissed his cheek. "Good night, Chase."

I heard the changing of the guards as I thought about all that had happened today. I heard Brad speak to the menfolk and let them know he would like three guards at a time, instead of two as he originally had suggested. He wanted to be sure that we were covered well around the camp and not stretched too thin.

The way we were taken care of, even on the hardest days, was comforting. The hard days and going to sleep hungry while snacking on dust seemed to fade away on days like today.

With the little Parker tucked into my wagon, I started to doze and wonder what tomorrow would bring. *G'night. Onward we go.*

Chapter Twenty-Six

Early morning came with the gray sky still lingering. Fires were fed lightly. We ate leftovers of biscuits and some other edibles that could be held and did not require washing up. Except for coffee and tea, of course.

As children were rising, the adults who were on watch duty were making sure coverage for those needing privacy would be accommodated as everyone readied for the day ahead.

Dennis told us that he, Jesse Gill, and Chase were headed to check the bear trap. He mentioned that he would need everyone to stay clear. As they started down the trail, in camp we heard the loudest bellow and then a horrendous roar. The three men crouched to listen and then took off at a run towards the loud roar with their guns ready.

Mothers grabbed the children that were up and out of their wagons, put them back in the wagons, and then jumped in themselves. Lots of commotion followed as folks prepared for a serious, life-threatening intrusion.

More loud noise, roaring, and thrashing of the brush continued to come from the location of the bear trap. The animal sounded incensed and full of rage. I was terrified, as were others. Men with guns pretty much surrounded the wagons, protecting the women, children, and animals. It was almost impossible to make a kill shot when a bear was charging. We were sure that this was a bear and that it was charging.

Dennis, being the first to see the huge bear with one leg in the trap, yelled to Jesse and Brad: "The trap might not hold him!"

Then he shot. The shot hit the thrashing bear in its front shoulder. It roared and yanked on the steel trap, trying to dislodge its huge leg. The shot made him madder, and he gave another fast and hard jerk, pulling the picket chain from the ground as he stood on his hind legs. At well over seven feet tall, he was massive. He was coming for anyone he could get his claws into. Making it count, Chase fired at his head as Jesse got him in his now-exposed chest.

The free bear stumbled, then stopped, and toppled over. The shot to the head had stopped him almost immediately, and the shot through the chest ensured it. The men waited a few minutes, assessing whether there was any chance that the bear was going to move or charge them. They knew that bears on all fours could move extremely fast for short distances, especially when angry or hurt; he could be both if still alive.

Once Dennis was satisfied that the bear was down and done for, he pulled his Bowie knife out and approached him, ready to fight up close if needed. If dead, he was ready to take him back to camp.

Dennis asked Chase to go get a couple of additional men to help carry the bear, which weighed more than 450 pounds, back to camp. Dennis would need help skinning as well.

Brad showed up with a couple more men. Together with Chase, Jesse, and Dennis, they carried the bear to camp. Dennis kidded that they could leave the bear bait, which was only half a fish at this point. The bear had managed to take the first bite as he stepped into the trap. They cleaned the trap out, and Dennis said that he would reset the trap before joining the camp. Chase stayed and helped him. According to Dennis, bears were somewhat territorial, so he did not think another bear would worry us in the area where we were now. But just in case, it would be set.

Once the bear was skinned out, Brad asked Dennis to cut it up so some of it could be jerked and the other used for our cooking pots. If it was used in the stewpot sparingly, there would be enough for everyone. It would take a couple of hours minimum to finish dressing out the bear. Dennis took the skin to tan. He said it would be great for the winter weather and keep him toasty warm.

Jesse asked Brad when he thought we would go back on the trail. Brad thought about it for a bit and said, "Let me get back to you in a bit." He muttered to himself as he walked toward the river with Dennis, Ben, and Rocky.

It was just shy of half an hour when Brad, Ben, and Rocky came back into camp. Brad called those of us who were close by together and announced that we would be staying here another night. He asked us to pass that on to our neighbors.

He said that with a river crossing in the next move, as well as the time it would take to dress out and divide up the bear, we would settle in for the day. He also mentioned that with any luck, more vittles might be available, sitting close by that river. The food would be much better in our stewpots than left behind. I didn't see one face in disagreement.

Laundry remained hanging under the wagons, and in some cases, more laundry was headed to the river with a couple of guards to assist. Cordelia and Kate had taken their jobs seriously and had received several reports back from folks on what their food supplies looked like. It was not looking good. The bear meat was surely a blessing.

As they went from wagon to wagon, they also let folks know that class would be midafternoon around two, instead of later, since we were not traveling today. It seemed like we were having another bright, eventful day, even with the damp, cold air. *Just goes to show that we are responsible for our own feelings and moods.*

I was pretty sure the animals were all feeling special right now, as they were getting more personal attention in the form of grain and lots of petting and cooing. Of course, it was the younger children and women mostly doing the cooing part of it.

The younger children were picking up more wood for tonight's fire and future fires. Until class started, the older ones picked more berries, paraffined the bottoms of water barrels, and helped where needed. Some worked on making traps, others were working on their slings. I did not notice anyone lounging except for Marsha Brahm. She looked all out, but not unhappy. She said she thought the babe was ready to join us anytime now. "I prefer to cross the river before the wee one arrives," she said.

I didn't think the time would be her choice, although lying still possibly helped a little to keep the babe in another day. We discussed that when the time came, she would let me know and would need my help. I told her to have one of her young'uns come and get me.

Before class today, stewpots with miniscule leftovers and fresh bear meat were added to the pots to simmer. Folks settled into the unhurried meal with comfort. Most had not had more than jerky for breakfast, so this was much appreciated.

We talked about tomorrow's crossing. Dennis said they had located another place to cross downstream a short distance. It was shallow, and the flow slowed down because of the bend in the river. When we pulled out tomorrow, Brad wanted us to pull out in the order of the lineup that he gave us. Jesse would lead off with the Ross family as previously discussed, then Titus driving Mrs. Linde's wagon, and so on.

"All children should be in a wagon, not walking," Brad said. "The water will only be up to the spokes of the wheels. However, with winter coming on, the water is frigid and could freeze your feet and legs if you're in the water too long."

Evelyn Linde would take control of her wagon once it was across the river. Brad mentioned that from here on, he was expecting Mrs. Linde to handle her own wagon. That would leave Titus and others free to assist everyone and do guard duty. Martin Linde had been guiding the Ross wagon oxen for some time. If needed, he would be the one to help his wife. "A reminder to all," Brad added, "don't forget your passengers and be ready to roll early."

Brad gave us good news tonight. We were looking at less than a month to reach our destinations. He couldn't give us an exact time, because it depended on the weather, accidents, intruders, and, of course, how far each one of us wanted to travel into the Oregon Territory.

"Some may find the further north they go," he said, "the better they like it. Others will fall in love when they see the southern exposure of the Oregon Territory."

Either way, he suggested that we talk with our families and do our planning. "Then," Brad said, "when we get to where you want to be, you pull out of the train, and you are home."

I took a deep breath. *I'm going to sit with Chase. I think we need to talk.* As I looked across the circle at Chase, he nodded to me, as if he had read my mind and was acquiescing. He stood and made for my wagon.

We talked in earnest for some time. He shared what he was looking for, but only after I told him, upon his request, what would make me feel at home in a new territory.

"I want to be married to a man who is honest and includes me in the planning of whatever we choose to do," I said. "A substantially-built home that is placed well on the land. It doesn't have to be big, but large enough to be comfortable for a family with two or three children. Preferably, live water, as the natives would say. That means running water from a creek or river, rather than a stale pond. Ground that can grow a crop other than rocks. One that we can run some animals on, preferably cattle, but it could be horses."

Then I told Chase more.

"Whatever my man is comfortable with will be fine," I said. "I want a generous man with affection for his children and his wife. One that is God-fearing and not ashamed to teach his children to be the same. I want to be able to stand side by side with my man and make our living count for something. I know these are big dreams for a woman just shy of girlhood. But I've already got one marriage behind me, and I'm sitting and looking at a second chance. I'm asking straight out for what I want now. If I don't ask, I won't get it, and it will be my own fault."

I watched Chase for a response.

I think he's up for the task. By the look in his eyes and pleased look on his face, he sure looks like he's ready and raring to try.

As Chase turned to face me close-up like, he stared into my eyes as he took my hands in his. He said, "Questa, I can't think of anyone, anywhere that I would rather live that life with. I want all the same things you do, and I'm about ready to bust out wanting to get there and get started."

Then he said, "I've never put much thought into what part of the territory I wanted to live in. Figured I would know when I saw it. With you helping me look, we're bound to find the perfect spot for us. Questa, please consider this as a proposal of marriage from me. Would you be my wife? Would you marry me as soon as we get to a preacher?"

I responded: "Chase Gunner, I'll marry you and be proud to be your wife. There's one problem though, as far as I can tell."

Chase's face froze. "What is it, Questa?"

"Well Chase, Brad is the wagon master, and he can bury us, and he can marry us. We could get married sooner if we have a mind to."

Chase touched my face and had the biggest smile.

"I hadn't thought of that," he said, "but sure would look forward to it whenever you're ready."

We both looked mighty silly smiling the way we were, just sitting there on the tongue of my wagon.

We talked more and decided we would wait until we found that piece of ground to homestead on. In the year of 1847, we would be included in the Distribution-Preemption Act of 1841, which gave settlers in the new territory the right to claim 160 acres of property. The settlers were required to live on the specific parcel of land for 14 months before becoming eligible to buy it for $1.25 per acre.[1] The United States government offered this incentive to help create a settlement during the westward movement that included us.

We would also benefit from a decision by the non-Native provisional government, which voted in 1843 that settlers had the right

---

1 HistoryLink.org, "Donation Land Claim Act, spur to American settlement of Oregon Territory, takes effect on September 27, 1850," by Margaret Riddle, Posted August 9, 2010; Essay 9501. https://historylink.org/File/9501 (last accessed December 28, 2020).

to claim up to 640 acres.[2] It seemed to me that either way, we were going to settle in the Oregon Territory. Furthermore, we could be at our new "home" within the month!

We walked, holding hands, down to see Brad and speak to him. We let him know that in case anything were to happen to one of us between now and when we settled, our intention was to be married, by him, and to take possession of each other's property as a married couple would. We wanted it to be witnessed, knowing that things happened that were out of our control just as they had already happened to me with Nalan's untimely death.

Brad shared with us that he had spoken with two other couples earlier about getting married as well. He smiled as he said that "love is in the air, and families are forming left and right." He did not tell us who they were, but we were pretty sure that Titus and Betha were one couple. We had seen them earlier gazing at each other, just like we had.

Kate and Cordelia asked me to walk with them to catch Brad for a discussion about available food stores within the 20 wagons. They looked a little down when they said the report was not good. Berries, wild onions, a little jerky, and flour—very little on the flour—were most of what was left. Hardly any sugar, coffee, or molasses was left. The ones most affected were, of course, the larger families with so many mouths to feed. Typically, they were driving the Conestoga wagons to allow for more food. There was an underestimation of what was needed with more attention being paid to what their oxen teams could actually pull. Speaking of the animals, without them we could not reach our destination. Brad reminded

____

2   HistoryLink.org, "Donation Land Claim Act, spur to American settlement of Oregon Territory, takes effect on September 27, 1850," by Margaret Riddle, Posted August 9, 2010; Essay 9501. https://historylink.org/File/9501 (last accessed December 28, 2020).

us often to make sure you paid close attention to their animal feed and to their care.

Everyone had been sharing very well when communal meals were taken. Brad said we would need to continue to do that to ensure that everyone was fed. We needed to take time to harvest as we proceeded. That would mean more traps needed to be set out at each camp. The catch of meat needed to be divided up, as it has been most of the trip, or at least the way it had been shared these last months.

Delia and Jack McCall relayed to us that while their laying hens held out, they would occasionally donate fresh eggs as well. It would mean that different families would benefit each time, since most likely there would never be more than six or eight eggs at once. The same distribution would happen with their milk, as long as we made sure the cow was fed enough to give milk. There were a couple of other milk cows on the train, and the same arrangement was made with them. Given the current food supplies, we have no more than a week's supply of food, not including the fresh food we harvested along the way. Our game was very important to our existence. Brad asked if some of the children could be given the task of grinding up the acorns that have dried to extend our flour reserves. Betha and Clara Robertson said they would organize that right away.

"Plan on being on the trail another month," Brad said, "although I hope it will be a shorter period of time."

We are all so hopeful.

Kate and Cordelia hurried back to the Wiggins wagon to prepare last-minute details for their students. They had decided to divide the class into those that could write and those that could not. They would go over the basics once again, including the spelling of each student's name and age. At that point, Cordelia would take those that could read. Kate would be responsible for those that could not read or write. They spaced their classes two wagons apart and began their second lesson.

The young faces had so much light and expectation in them. Kate's students were so excited that they were learning to read and write and do figures. A couple of the children brought a piece of paper. It was used on one side, but it still gave them one side to work on, which was better than nothing. They had what was left of a small stub of a pencil. The brother and sister shared the paper and the pencil. One student had a slate that his older brother had used at one time. His brother felt it was more important that his younger sibling have it, since he was just learning his letters and numbers, and it could be used over and over. He also had a slate pencil with one edge wrapped tightly with a small cloth. A cloth for cleaning his slate was also attached to the bottom of the board, so as not to become separated from the slate.

Cordelia's class was moving at a faster rate because the students had previous learning opportunities. Between Cordelia, Kate, and Tanner, there were four different books for the students to share and read. They started with the easiest novel, passed it around, and took turns reading it. The hour passed swiftly with the students not wanting to stop. For the most part, they were hungry to learn. Three of Kate's students had mastered writing their names, both first and last, as well as their ages. They were thrilled!

How proud I am of these girls for taking interest in their fellow travelers and teaching these children. These same children will enter a new time in the west and will escort self-confidence with them.

During a stroll beside wagons, I noticed excited students continuing to practice outside of the classroom. They were using a long stick to write on the ground wherever possible.

After a bit, Rush Spencer came along with a smile. He held up a possum that he had caught in his trap. He said he wanted to donate it to the Brahms if that was fine with Brad. Why he was telling me I was not sure, since it surely wouldn't be up to me. But I acknowledged that notifying Brad would be the thing to do.

He sure acted different over the last months of travel. I could almost forgive him for his earlier behavior, but not quite. I knew I needed to work on forgiveness of my fellow man. My Momma and Papa both used to say that I had a mite of a stubborn streak in me. *I don't think I was that bad. I just know what is right and what is wrong. Nevertheless, I'll put my mind to working a bit harder on forgiveness.*

At suppertime, our fires were welcoming, especially knowing that we had a nice stew coming tonight made up of leftovers with fresh bear meat. Other traps had been placed throughout the day but were empty, except for the fish in a couple of the river traps. Brad said the animal traffic is slow next to the river during the day because of all the traffic we have created. Tomorrow morning chances were that they would look different.

Several of our menfolk had set traps along the river that they had recently made themselves. Others brought a trap with them, and wise they were. We were especially grateful for the bear trap.

Marsha Brahm came from the wagon for a bit and asked if I would walk with her for some privacy. She looked so uncomfortable and had stayed very close to her wagon all day. Her oldest girls, being 11 and 12, had pretty much been her shadow and a good help to their Ma. I could see that they had assisted her with getting the back of the wagon prepared for the upcoming birth. But she asked her girls to stay at the wagon rig while we went to take care of our private woman time.

Marsha shared that with this being child number six, it would come quickly. She was trying to anticipate. She said that even now, she had hot water on the fire in case she started her labor. "If it's a girl, I want her to be called Allison," she said. "If it's a boy, he's to be called Simon. Jozeph and I are in agreement on the names."

We both found a private area to do our business. It was hard for Marsha to stand back up with her large extended stomach, and she asked me for help as she exhaled deeply. We started away from the bushes, and Marsha stopped and groaned loudly. Water pooled around her feet. Her water had broken, and she had started her labor. I called quietly for her husband Jozeph who was our guard. Together, we gave Marsha the support she needed to get back and into the wagon.

We made sure all the children were out from under the wagon or in the back of it. Jozeph and their sons, Elisha and Jess, had rigged up a good lean-to while it was still light out. Jozeph let Brad know he was off duty while his wife was birthing his new son or daughter.

Just as Marsha had said it probably would, the labor and the delivery were moving right along. I had Jozeph get us a large pan of hot water. The girls had already gathered clean rags as well as a change of clothes for Marsha, a gown, a swaddling blanket, and several nappies for the baby. On a clean cloth on the side of a box next to where Marsha was lying down, a pair of scissors and alcohol were ready.

I was scared. I remembered all too well that first and last birth I helped with, and holding the beautiful, lifeless body of little Margaret Parker.

Oh Lord, I know you're there, and you hear me. Please help me do this right and give both mother and child the help they need. Don't let anything happen to take either of their lives. We would miss them so. Thank you, Lord.

Some two hours later with little more than muttering from Marsha, she delivered little Simon Brahm. What a healthy little guy. He came out hungry and ready to talk. In fact, I think if we had handed him a fishing pole, he would have taken it to the water and caught our supper.

He latched onto her breast pretty quickly after a little help from Marsha, who dipped her finger into milk and touched his little mouth with it. Once he started, he didn't want to stop.

While she cuddled and fed the little guy, I cleaned up her and Simon. I gave the water to Jozeph to dump and also gave him room to be next to his wife and new son while they admired each other. The children, outside under the tarp, had quieted down and fell right to sleep. Jozeph would join them once his wife had nodded off.

I lay in bed that night thinking about how I would be starting a family with Chase someday. I was smiling as I fell asleep. We would roll in the morning.

Chapter Twenty-Seven

THE COLD AIR WAS waiting the next morning. It had touched the tops of everything, including our water barrels. We all had to break the layer of ice in our water barrels to dip out water for coffee and tea. Luckily, the night before I had once again covered the backs of my oxen and given them as much hay as I could rightly afford. I was ever aware that without our oxen and horses, we would not make it. It was a job keeping their strength up as well as our own. We were constantly reminded to pay special attention to the weather. It was a barometer for the amount and the type of food we needed to keep them healthy and moving forward.

That was not saying that their food sources were not depleting, because they were. We'd been fortunate to find some grass the past several days. That helped. We didn't have to depend solely on the little hay that we did have. As we went forward though, we have been told there would be some time in the very near future that we would be rolling over rock walls and valleys where no grass existed. We could ill afford to lay up again, continuing to use our food reserves, and not moving closer to our destination.

We were now using our coffee grounds more than once a day. Our coffee was weaker of course, but its warmth and the milder flavor got us through until our one meal of the day, which was during our evening stop. The children were an exception; we made sure they had some sustenance when we started out in the morning. Occasionally the adults would get a boiled egg if enough were available. Or maybe a spoonful of stew, if any was left over from the evening meal. We also made sure Marsha Brahm had something to eat to get her started in the mornings. She was nursing and needed the food to sustain herself and baby Simon.

I rubbed my animals down again before hitching them up with Chase's help. The others did the same. When we leave today our new wagon lineup would be with Chase in the number seven position, and I would be in the ninth. As we were readying my oxen, he made sure to tell me that if I needed him at any point, like crossing the river, I should just say the word, and he would be right there.

He gives me such hope that traveling away from my family and everything I am familiar with to a foreign territory is going to work out just fine for us. We agreed; we will do this together. That is such a comfort.

While the menfolk were checking traps this morning, others were on guard duty. Once my wagon was hitched up, I made a cup of tea and went to see Marsha Brahm and the new little Simon Brahm. Marsha would be riding in the wagon all day again today in order to tend to Simon. The children would be in their designated wagons while we were crossing the river. In case they were needed to keep the oxen focused on the other bank, Rocky and Ben made ready to ride their horses on either side of each team of oxen as they crossed the river. Brad did not see a need for them to escort each wagon. It would mean keeping the feet of their horses in the freezing cold water the entire time that it took for the 20 wagons to cross. However, they would stay close to the loose livestock as they crossed.

As he woke, Simon's sweet baby face rooted around for the smell and feeling of his mother's comfort. It was not for the first time during the night. Marsha and I talked while she had her cup of tea and nursed little Simon briefly. At this point, he didn't eat that much, but Marsha explained that in a day or so his appetite would increase significantly. She asked me if I wouldn't mind fixing her canteen so she could have it nearby her once they rolled. She would need to drink adequate liquids to help her milk supply. I was happy to do that.

While I was there, Delia McCall showed up with a gallon of fresh milk. We were so excited. I quickly poured Marsha a cup of milk, which she savored. Each of the children and Jozeph also had a cup of milk. We stored the remaining milk under the front seat of the wagon wedged between a block of wood and blankets that were not moving. We were hoping that it wouldn't be too rough while traveling and churn it into butter. It was a real treat for them, along with the half dozen eggs she brought. We scrambled the eggs, adding a little of the fresh milk and divvied them up to each of the Brahm family members. Marsha tried to get me to share with them, and I told them that I had already eaten. Which I had, though the small palmful of seeds I ate had worn off within minutes of eating them.

I held little Simon as Marsha took some time for herself with Jozeph watching over her closely.

The menfolk were coming back to the wagons very excited. The traps had been very successful the past night.

A number of fish and rabbits were in the set traps, as well as a possum in the bear trap. Very early this morning, before the noise from our camp had disrupted them, a couple of deer were shot while they were drinking from the river. It was so helpful that we had numerous traps out. I credited Dennis for showing others how to make and set them, and the best places and times to put them out. This was a skill that each one of us needed to know.

Chase and I had asked Dennis if sometime soon he would show us how to build the traps. He was a very busy man with so many skills that benefited us. I had started working on my moccasins and needed to step up my efforts so that I had them finished before my boots were completely worn through the soles.

This morning I put a couple of handfuls of dried grass in the soles of my boots. It was a way to keep your feet warmer. Another of those tricks that Dennis had taught us. He said it was a method that the Indians used. Moccasins wore out faster than our boot soles, and they were not as warm. It was good to know that I needed to always be aware of the usage left in a pair of shoes, whether they were boots or moccasins.

Dennis told me and Chase that he wouldn't have much time for the next week because of scouting and such. However, he suggested that Chase get together with Titus and a couple of the other men-folk so that they could show him how to make a trap, then Chase could show me. Dennis had already set some time tomorrow night to work with several of the folks to teach them how to make moccasins. He was also bringing some skins for the shoes.

We both immediately said we would follow his suggestion. I realized we were both excited about learning something new that was going to improve our lives. It made me more aware of what a great idea it was to have the children on the trip attending school as we traveled westward. It made me think about my own education. I was 15 when Nalan and I married and my formal education ended. Tanner, Cordelia, and Kate were younger and older than me, respectively, but obviously, they had a better education than I did. *I will ask Cordelia tonight if I can sit in on her daily class when I have the time.*

Folks were on their own as far as finding something to eat for breakfast. Most just had some chicory coffee because our other coffee was exhausted. The stew was pretty well scraped off the bottom of the stewpots, leaving only a memory of last night's hot meal.

Today's treasure from the traps would be for dinner tonight. We would share once again after the day was through, and we had settled for the night. For now, we were getting our wagons lined up to leave our campsite.

Anytime you crossed a river, there were additional perils to be concerned about. However, knowing that we were crossing in a shallow part of the river was so helpful. It also helped that Brad had mentioned last night that we were within a month of finding our homes. We were all so hopeful and so cold.

Rocky and Ben were walking their horses down the line and getting the wagons in the back that would be moved closer up to the front. They were assisting with getting the additional cattle and horses across the river without tying them to the back of a wagon, creating one less hazard for the crossing.

Jesse and Almira Gill led off, followed by the Ross family. Then came Evelyn Linde's wagon driven by Titus until he crossed the river, then the driving was Evelyn's responsibility. Others followed, abiding by the lineup that had been previously decided with Rush Spencer happily in the number four position. Chase was number seven in the lineup, and I was number nine. Daniel and Josephine Dawson, a couple with no children, were the last in the train. They did have chickens and a plow horse, though. Something that I had been unaware of before the lineup changed. That was another reason to change the order of the train more than once. You got acquainted with others on the trip. You began to know their setup and what their dreams were.

In all, we were 20 wagons. Thus far, we had lost one wagon and gained one since I joined the group. We were now one big family and were striving to reach the end with everyone in good health. Although, we were a little "lighter on the hoof and in the britches."

We crossed the river without any major issues. As previously decided, we redistributed the children, or those riding in the wagon, to walking or riding. Then we continued on.

The oxen warmed up and put their bodies into the day ahead. They had been given a little grain this morning, along with their rubdown and hay. They had eaten better than most of us.

I'm not sure how the catches from the traps were taken care of this morning, but I am sure they were stored somewhere until we had time to stop and skin out. It's cold enough that there won't be any spoilage. However, a thought did cross my mind: can other animals catch the scent of what we are carrying?

That night in camp we had school, and I did attend. Others skinned out our early morning catch and reset our traps. We were not near water tonight but had found a wonderfully flat area with a little grass and lots of wild edibles, such as sage, onions, and a few camas. There were still some huckleberries, but not many of them, as we were well past fall and moving quickly into winter, as our weather was stridently reminding us.

We had another communal supper tonight with stewpots simmering a variety of meat, acorn flour for thickening, wild onions, and a few dried squashes. We saved other dried vegetables for another time. We had no guarantees that we would continue to reap the benefits of our traps. We were all famished after traveling all day with little or no sustenance. Sometimes the younger children complained of hunger. We made sure they had something at breakfast. That had to hold them until the supper meal, whatever that turned out to be. Combined efforts brought forth enough flour for biscuits, enough so that each person had half a biscuit to go along with their stew.

With the cold increasing again tonight, we followed a plan of rubbing down our animals, covering the ones that could be covered, and making sure they had hay and some grain to keep their backs up to the chore of pulling our lives in a box.

Luckily, we woke to our traps having good catches, although nothing like what we had experienced near the river the prior evening. The deer, fish, and rabbits were welcome but they were very lean. Our bodies needed fat to keep us healthy. Each day I could see the difference in our families, as they got sparer and sparer. For certain, we were thankful to have the catches, whatever they were. It was food, and it sustained us. Our wagons became lighter as we became lighter. It was too bad that the few little plants I brought had had no time to bear any potatoes or apples during the trip. I hoped they would live long enough to be planted in Oregon once we have settled.

The distance we made today wasn't bad; it was just the never-ending plodding along. It was one day closer to the end. Wherever the "end" was. We were racing against time now. Some said they could smell the snow ready to fall. Dennis said it didn't snow much here. However, the cold bit just as bad, especially in the mountains. Everyone who had extra bedding has long since pulled it out and was using it. Tarps had become a must, not only to keep out the rain, but also the heavy frost that plagued us each night.

I'm fortunate to be able to sleep in my wagon and have a little person warming the space as well.

That night, school was not only in session when we camped, but I was also able to join some of the others for a lesson in how to make moccasins. Chase and some of the other menfolk joined in for a short time as well. They left early to join other men in making traps. We both felt that both skills were going to be very important to us in the future, on and off the wagon train.

Now we can trade knowledge. I'm so excited about Chase's willingness to share in our future decisions, beginning with educating ourselves and picking out the right place to settle together.

For the next several days, we traveled up and down hillsides and across flats. One mountain in particular took us up and over a pretty steep pass and down the other side to a grassy meadow next to a creek. It was a tough crossing, but it was not considered treacherous compared to some of the others we had previously crossed. What was treacherous was the sign of Indians once we had settled for the night.

We circled the wagons with the animals in the center. School was still held near the Wiggins wagon, now number 12 in the lineup. We had communal cook pots. Everyone served themselves and then returned to their wagons, keeping a loaded gun at the ready. Guards were set for the night. Everyone was told there would be no music of any kind and no going off for private time without a guard.

We were keeping the fires low tonight and making sure that our horses and milk cows were staked and hobbled, making it tougher to steal them. We had all been told that our canteens should be filled and worn on our person in case we were attacked and separated from our water barrel. We could live without food for a time, but not water.

Brad informed us that he thought we were near a gravesite of the wagons that came through in 1846. A young lady had died of typhoid fever. Later the Indians desecrated her grave. He was not sure if there had ever been an Indian battle there, but from the moccasin prints, he could see that obviously there were some around. For that reason, he said, "We should be on constant alert."

I checked with Marsha Brahm to see if she needed anything. She was getting around well, and little Simon seemed to grow by the minute. He appeared satisfied and well-adjusted to his life in a wagon. The other children were well-behaved and did what they could to help. Though it was important to keep in mind that they were small children. Sometimes, actually most of the time, they could be a handful, especially with a new baby. But Marsha seemed content as well. At night she slept in the wagon with baby Simon and five-year-old Isabella. Jozeph slept outside with the other four children under the wagon and the tarp. Jozeph had reminded all his family to stick close to the wagon and always be together.

The place where we camped tonight was actually in a lovely opening between the mountain we had just crossed and another substantial crossing in front of us. Before bed tonight, Brad had everyone pick up some jerked venison for lunch tomorrow, and he made sure our guns were loaded.

I picked more grass for my boots tonight before it got frosted again. I also added some to the youngest Robertson and Parker shoes. *Heaven knows their mothers have their hands full.*

Brad called a quick camp meeting and let everyone know we were preparing to go up through the Umpqua Canyon. This was an extremely rocky area that was impassable unless we had two spare weeks to work our way through. We didn't have the time or the food resources to do that. He said that we would be using a trail that Dennis scouted. It was a combination of the Jedediah trappers trail and the Applegate. According to what has been passed along to Brad, there was no ideal trail here. We were looking for the most accessible and quickest route possible. Sometimes the two didn't come together.

The conversation always seemed to revert back to the Indians. We knew that more than one tribe lived near the Umpqua River. Indians had taken saddle horses in the past; we had known that from the beginning. Once again, we were warned to be on the ready.

Those with eggs boiled them that night and made them available the next morning, starting with the children, and then continuing until they ran out. Jerky would be given to those who did not get an egg. The milk cows were not giving as much milk because they were not getting fed as much as their bodies needed to keep producing.

It was suggested that night that everyone take a spoonful of vinegar to guard against scurvy. Some have been doing it, but others disliked the taste, so they ignored it. Other than onions, we were not getting enough fresh vegetables in our diet and were not likely to for some time.

Traps were set out surrounding the outside of the wagons where the traffic was at a minimum. Five guards were placed around the outside circle of the wagons.

Today some Camas roots were found. They were nutritious but very hard on delicate digestions and caused extreme discomfort if not cooked properly. There was also more than one type of Camas. The Blue Camas was good. The other, the White or "death" Camas was not. Dennis showed us how to recognize the good one and warned us that we need to be ever cautious about the plant we dug up.

"The roots of the edible plant need to be cooked underground for three days," he said. "They must be cleaned off and a hole dug for them to be covered with hot, smoldering ashes in a portion of the campsite. In our case, we will have to dig them up every day and rebury them each evening in the new campsite until they are cooked. Otherwise, we can count on extremely upset stomach, gas, and diarrhea."

I'm not sure that this is something any one of us wants to try out. As we get hungrier though, we may change our minds.

Chase and I were sitting on a bucket and the tongue of my wagon when Titus and Betha came by tonight, just before the curtain of night covered us. They were as excited as Chase and I are about reaching Oregon. They confirmed that they were the other couple that had also talked to Brad about their future plans. They even talked about the possibility of us being neighbors. Having another young couple that we already knew living close by would be such a treat. We were rolling out early tomorrow. *I'm not sure what we will face but I know that I will need my rest.* Chase kissed me on my hand and then lightly on my cheek before wishing me a good night.

Chapter Twenty-Eight

UPON WAKING EARLIER THAN normal, I found a restlessness among all of us. Several were out of their bedrolls and beds, getting fires going, and starting hot coffee. The cold was going right through us. Even though we had had no snow during the night, it was so cold that my bones hurt. Others were rubbing their arms and hands to get the circulation going. Jozeph and Marsha and other parents with very young children were checking them to make sure they had all survived the night. Luckily, at times children seemed to be more resilient than their parents. Even baby Simon, who was wrapped especially warm, was oblivious to the cold.

Before I came out of the wagon, I put on my extra pair of socks and left the grass in my boots for added warmth. I would be walking today and that would help to warm me.

Most of us had to break the ice on our water barrels before putting water into buckets for our livestock. Once I did that, I barely warmed a bucket of water for my oxen. They needed water, but not so cold that their insides would hurt. Because our animals were so lean and getting leaner by the hour due to rationing their food, it was important to do what we could to help them keep warmer on these cold days. Especially given the hard work that we were asking of them. As Nellie and Locks drank their water and had their hay and grass mix, I rubbed them down, their legs included. They were quite content when they got the extra attention. It made me feel better to make the effort.

The traps were fairly successful last night. A number of smaller animals were caught and then skinned out this morning. They were ready for cooking tonight at the end of the trail. I had forgotten that I had a handful of dried beans, as did Marsha and others. We combined them in three pots of water to soak today while we traveled. We would cook them tonight in time for the following day. They would give us a little of that fat we needed in our bodies and didn't get from our lean animal catches.

As folks moved around and got ready to travel, there was an expectancy of a rougher trail up ahead. Brad said it might be another day or two, although we were starting up to higher ground again, which could be colder. He was pretty sure it would be tougher to get through.

The history of this area was that the previous travelers had to do much of their own clearing. Dennis had been asked to go ahead and take Titus, his gun, and the machete. They were to give us a report of what they found, as well as clear small barriers when possible, and always be on the lookout for Indians.

Once the first wheel rolled, there was little conversation. The children had their boiled eggs. Others had a biscuit, or whatever edible was available. Time was split between driving from the wagon seats and leading from the side while walking. It was a good way to break the routine when allowable by the terrain. The smaller children stayed in the wagons for most of the day, but that afternoon they had to expend some energy by walking for about an hour. They did slow the train, however, so Brad had them back in their wagons after only the one hour, which seemed to be just right. I rode in the afternoon as well. I could hear the two little ones who rode with me giggling in the back of the wagon and practicing their ABCs that they were learning in the early evening class in camp. It was priceless and gave me so much hope for their future.

We traveled until the sun rose and then stuttered in the sky before descending for the day. I quickly put my beans on the fire, as well as the stewpot that Marsha had somehow put together on the road. As they cooked, I took care of my oxen. Chase had helped me with removing their hitching gear. I checked the beans and stew and tidied up my two young passengers before we headed to the Wiggins wagon to attend our respective classes.

For an hour, I lost myself in our readings and the discussions that followed. We were in different levels of our education, but it didn't matter. We all knew we wanted to learn more and could do so by sharing the experience.

Cordelia Base was 19 years old and our teacher. She had three younger siblings. One of them, 14-year-old Leta, was also in our class. Cordelia had long golden hair; she was tall and very outspoken, although not impolite. We discovered that she had gone as far as she could in school and then had worked as a teacher's assistant in an academy of higher learning for boys. At this time, there were no schools of higher learning available for girls in Missouri.

She learned from listening, watching, and assisting in grading assignments as directed by the teacher. She was not paid as the assistant, other than the exposure to the classroom, and that was exactly what we were getting from Cordelia.

In addition to being bright and helpful, Cordelia and Solomon Whittacker had become quite close and would probably marry sometime down the way.

We all supped that night on stew from our early morning catch. The camp was devoid of music. Besides remaining aware of the potential threat of Indians, the musicians had cold hands as the temperatures continued to drop.

Last night when we made moccasins, Dennis showed us something we could do for more protection against the cold. We used some of the skins as an arm protector. The skin fastened from the top of the hand up to the elbows. It could be worn over our coat sleeves or under, whichever way worked best for us. It was laced up and tied. Leggings could also be made for the same purpose but the skin had to be bigger. I made an arm set for myself and started two smaller sets for my little passengers.

We were called emigrants, pioneers, and oxmen. The truth was that it didn't matter what they called us, especially if we didn't make it to the end of the trail. What did matter was that we embraced what we were learning to make our lives safer, or more comfortable, or longer. In order to do that, we had to use our time wisely and survive.

Chase worked on his trap in silence as I worked on my moccasins tonight. I broke that silence and asked Chase to tell me more about himself, and he began.

He was 25. Until he was 17, he attended school while working as an assistant bookkeeper at a mill. His parents died when he was 17, and he needed a full-time job that paid better to support himself. He was hired to work on a local cattle ranch where he learned everything about cattle ranching that he could. He turned no job down. He mucked the stalls and did the milking, branding, and roundups. He slept in the bunkhouse with a pretty rascally bunch of cowpokes for almost three years. They taught him how to fight, handle a gun, and build a house. They also taught him how to judge a man and avoid trouble when needed or how to jump in with both feet, spurs, and all when needed.

He was unaware that his folks had pretty much lost their place before they died. A fact he had to deal with after they passed away. He got rid of most of the farm equipment, except for a buckboard, pulling horses, and his personal things. He kept an adze and other small building implements. He put his money into an account in town and made arrangements with his new employer to keep his two horses and equipment on his place. Later, he ended up selling the buckboard and pulling horses and getting a saddle horse instead. He taught it to be his cutting horse.

After three years, he decided he wanted to use his construction experience, and he set off to find the right opportunity. It actually turned out to be right there in his hometown. The town was growing rapidly. Many new businesses were popping up in Missouri to accommodate the folks congregating there. Many had hopes of moving westward; others just hoped to get rich off those moving west. Either way, they needed help in building their stores, law offices, and newspaper offices.

Chase was available and fair in his pricing. As fast as he could finish one place, he would be hired for the next job. Sometimes even before he finished the job he was working on. He did good work, and the word traveled fast. He continued to save his money in his account in town and lived in a boarding house that was fairly priced and served two good meals a day.

His construction business would have kept him busy seven days a week forever, but Chase felt he had more to learn. He cut his construction business down to three days a week, took Sundays off for church, and went to work for a blacksmith the other three days a week. "Why a blacksmith?" I asked.

He told me that since he was 17 and found himself alone without a home and family, his dream had been to move west, build a home, and start a cattle ranch. To do that, he needed to know ranching, construction, and how to take care of his animals. He set to it, and was moving west with all his dreams.

Actually, his dreams are more than being realized. He met me, fell in love, and can't wait to reach our new home together.

When I think back about our previous conversations, I realize that we are a perfect match for one another.

I could not miss this opportunity to lean in to Chase, while laying my hands in his, and kissing him lightly, but square on his mouth.

He went to his wagon with a smile and good night on his lips.

I had used my private time wisely along with Marsha Brahm. She checked on her little ones when we returned from relieving ourselves, and we said our good nights.

As expected, the cold pervaded again last night. However, everyone had taken extra precautions against the cold and seemed in good spirits. As long as it didn't rain on us, and we didn't run out of food for ourselves, or for our animals, we would manage. Even if the cold was uncomfortable.

Leftovers and jerky were breakfast fare. Hot coffee for us with warm milk or water for the children, depending on what their family had access to. The animals were given water that had been warmed briefly. We followed the same routine as the day before. The Camas bulbs were dug up once again. Tonight would be the last night for them to be roasted and added to our diets. If placed on the fire as soon as we settled tonight, the beans would be ready for our supper.

Traps were checked again with the fresh catch to be taken care of when we stopped this afternoon for a break.

We rolled out the next morning. It was bitterly cold. The ascent was not steep, but noticeable. We had to take a couple of rests the first four hours on the trail. Dennis and Titus had gone ahead of us and used the machete where needed. There was proof that other wagons had crossed this area before us in years past. Their tracks would sometimes disappear for many hours, meaning that we had taken a different course at times. We were taking the route that Dennis and Titus were marking. Our trust at this point was in our gut and in our wagon master, Brad.

We were thinking about every meal now and every step that the oxen were ambulatory. So many had gone before us and without nearly as positive an experience. I knew that the Applegate brothers said this was an easier course of travel than what they experienced in 1843 on the Oregon Trail. I also knew that there were others on that previous train that were noted to have said that was not necessarily true of this "southern route." That was the biggest reason that I felt better following our own guides. They had already proven themselves over and over.

I overheard Evelyn and Martin Linde talking this morning, and she was complaining that she was not comfortable driving her wagon by herself. Martin told her that starting tomorrow, he would manage the wagon and the ox. Depending on the terrain, she would be walking most of the time. *With little food in her belly and an uphill climb,* I thought, *she may soon sing another tune.*

We continued our slow but steady progress and at midday we started to level off. According to Brad, the descent would begin soon. We stopped once all wagons were on level ground and took a break. Folks found places to relieve themselves, checked their animals and wagons, took a breath, and those who had been walking took a short sit down. Young'uns hugged their parents and grabbed as much attention as they could. Some had saved whatever edible they had from breakfast and ate it now. The traps were emptied out, and the catches were skinned by each trap owner.

We were on top of a mountain, but it was brushy, so we couldn't see far at all. This must have been part of the problem when the first emigrants came this way. However, those who came before us had done some clearing for us. In other places that we went, we bypassed each other.

Over an hour later, Brad told us to start moving again, keeping in mind that we were going downhill.

"Keep your wagon slow but steady," he said. "It's a nice, long, easy descent, so it shouldn't harm man or beast."

All of us, except for Evelyn Linde, had no problems or complaints. She stopped at one point going down the grade and refused to go further. She cried and fluffed her hands around while making terrible faces. The girls who had ridden with her tried to calm her, but to no avail. Her husband Martin Linde, who was helping with the Ross wagon in front of them, took over.

Evelyn had had a pretty easy life up until the move westward. A move that I understood she did not want to go on. Her husband made that decision. That, coupled with being hungry, cold, and having already lost all their possessions, had just been too much for her.

Besides Evelyn, Rush Spencer had been dealing with a toothache since he woke this morning. It got to the point up on the mountain that he couldn't concentrate to manage his team. Tanner Wiggins came forward to manage it as Rush stumbled along moaning and holding his face between his hands. There were no headache powders or pain medicines left for him. It was certain that he needed the tooth out as quickly as possible.

Since he said the pain couldn't be any worse, he agreed to allow Marsha to remove his tooth.

A bucket was brought to the side of his wagon, and a large cloth wrapped around his throat and tied behind his neck. A long strand of thread made of deer gut was wrapped around the base of the offending tooth. The hardest part was wrapping the string around the tooth without getting bitten. Marsha turned, as if she had to get something else, and with the tooth wrapped tightly with the string, she jerked her arm fast and hard. Rush grunted loudly as the tooth sailed from his mouth. He was immediately given a splash of salt water to rinse with before Marsha quickly packed the cavity where the tooth no longer resided. He crawled into his wagon and rested there until we stopped that evening. His groaning had stopped.

For at least three days, we traveled up and down passes, catching small animals in our traps, and taking turns walking and riding. We cared for our animals and tried to stay warm. We had our classes and our traps and moccasins, making to keep us forever occupied.

Dennis and Titus had gone on ahead of us. They did not return until they had the route for the next several days figured out. In the meantime, they had marked the route for us as they went to avoid getting us caught in a one-way canyon or some such thing. We saw many places along the way where other trains had divided and gone in different directions. We had decided early on that we would follow Brad's lead, and his lead was to follow Dennis and Titus.

So far, we were still finding food and surviving the cold. Tonight, a nasty drizzle had started, making it impossible to stay dry, meaning it would be impossible to stay warm. We all pulled out canvases and made lean-tos by parking the wagons end-to-end or side-by-side and stretching the canvases from wagon to wagon. We were hoping that by doing it early, the ground would not be too soaked to sleep on. As long as it didn't pour, it would work well.

Class was conducted under tarps, and we ate our small supper under tarps as well.

The Camas bulbs were roasted well tonight. A couple of the men with stout stomachs tried the bulbs with their beans. I didn't know how they would tell the difference in what causes any gas or digestion issues they might experience. *I'm glad I have no men in my camp tonight.*

There would be no blankets on the oxen tonight because the rain would soak them and make them ineffective. Besides, with the rain, the temperature had actually improved. We are another day closer to our new lives.

Stay with us, Lord. Deliver us safely to our new lives. Amen.

Chapter Twenty-Nine

SLEEP OVERTOOK THOSE NOT on guard duty tonight. We were worn out cumulatively as well as by today's travel and everything that accompanied it.

As the mountains loomed in front of us, we realized that we had to somehow penetrate this obstruction. And it was an obstruction, made of pure rock. Dennis and Titus were somewhere up ahead of us, marking the best route. Even with solid rock, we were certain of an opening because a creek ran out of the south side of the rock, and besides, others had passed before us. *Are we that off the original trail crossing?*

We followed the signs that Dennis left for us. Somehow, we continued to move forward, although in close enough confines that we had to get in front of our wagons or ride because there was no room to walk alongside the wagon.

There was a strange echo as the wagons moved through the rocks. We proceeded, not knowing if we would be ambushed or die there, starved and stuck between mammoth rock walls.

Following the signs from Dennis kept us on our toes and staring ahead, and to the sides of us, all the time. Many times, we found ourselves barely moving as we pressed through the narrow crevasses and rolled inch by inch, stiltedly, over the rock. Dennis and Titus did come back to us the second night after we had made it through the rock canyon to the other side, which took us nigh on a full three days.

On the second night when Dennis and Titus showed up, they came bearing gifts: two deer that they had shot. The deer had been foraging, and they were not considered big or fat, but they tasted excellent. Along with dried squash, onions, and the Camas roots, that were looking better all the time, we felt thankful and not nearly as hungry as we had been. Several folks with young'uns had also been given eggs in the last couple of days.

The deer were great and unexpected. Even more unexpected was a pack that Titus carried. They had found a disabled wagon with household items that had been abandoned on one of the other trails they scouted. In it they found canned goods, including peaches and green beans. The couple dozen cans were pure gold to every one of us. Brad had them stored in the Linde buckboard with instructions that they were not to be opened or given to anyone. They would be saved for a night when we had nothing else or for a celebration of sorts.

The drizzle of rain had stayed with us off and on. But always sufficiently on to make our misery twofold: both hungry and now wet. I thought about my feelings and felt ashamed. If the little ones learned early on that it was no good to complain, then I also would not complain.

On the third day, we came out of the canyon. If only the sun had been shining, it would have looked like heaven. But it was enough to make everyone smile.

We stopped for a while and checked our wagons. We were close to a river, so we filled our canteens and water barrels once again. Then off we rolled. Many of us chose to walk again, after being cooped up in the wagon for the last couple of days, and to give the oxen a break from our added weight. The wagons rolled on until late afternoon when we finally struck camp. Once again, we had room to circle the wagons and prepare communal meals.

We held our classes, folks made sure that their animals were treated with extra care, and tarps were stretched wagon to wagon where possible. Fish traps were set in a creek nearby, as were traps for small animals. We were reminded that we had more rock to pass through so, if at all possible, we needed to stock up on fresh game. It was suggested that we check our traps once in the evening and again in the morning.

Two wheels on the Gill's wagon had some damage, and he set right to work getting them fixed. Their wagon being the first in the lineup, he had not been aware of a large boulder hidden beneath the soil. It jostled him and his wife Almira quite a bit. Almira was thrown around enough to bite her lip and bruise her arm badly. Jesse stopped the wagon immediately, and got them resituated with Jesse walking in front of the oxen. He needed to be able to spot future problems on the trail and make other wagons aware of them. The help of some of the others allowed him to repair the wheel in preparation for their continuation tomorrow.

It occurred to many of the women that it had been a very long time since we, or our families, had bathed. We agreed that it was way too cold to go into the creek, but we were capable of warming water and surrounding each other while we took turns bathing. In addition to depending on each other, a couple of the menfolk helped put up a hasty covering for us to undress and dress behind. We had a couple more tubs outside of our hasty dressing room for those who felt brave enough to wash their hair.

Some of the children had been battling with head lice and needed some reprieve. I honestly didn't know how the bugs survived as dirty as the hair of some of the children appeared to be. Many of the children and the men had not done any handwashing since the last river. *I guess they have never heard that "cleanliness is next to godliness."* There were people on the train who believed that washing the dirt off could make them sick because they would have no protection against the elements. They thought that clean skin did not provide the barrier they needed.

Once we were done, the water was changed out for any of the men inclined to clean up. A couple of them, including Chase, even shaved. I noticed that three of them got noticeable hair and beard trims.

Folks were glad to be through the rocks tonight. However, the exhaustion was taking its toll on man and animals. Chase and I discussed that very thing tonight. We were ready to start our new lives together and would have a very open mind as we traveled further north in the Oregon Territory. If the land were rightly situated and within a reasonable distance of a town or other folks, we would consider it rather than going to the end of the Applegate Trail.

That night and the next morning brought more catch in our traps. Enough to provide us a communal dinner for the next two nights. Some had fish in their traps that they ate for breakfast this morning. Others had jerky to get them through the day until supper.

Rolling hills and winding paths took us upward again until we realized we faced another rock wall. After managing the prior rock obstruction and managing to get all of us through it, we girded ourselves up, and we trusted.

Onward we went, following the trail that Dennis and Titus left us for the next day and a half. Early afternoon on the second day, we came through the other side. This time, we were not as worn out from the worry of not knowing as we were before. By the time we came out of the rock that day, a blustery, cold, slanted rain came down, not leaving a dry spot anywhere on our person. We rolled until midafternoon. Then we stopped and stretched canvases over us and on the sides of the wagons wherever we could manage it. We found a large, thick stand of pine trees that seemed to be dryer at the base than anywhere else. Many laid their beds there for the night. Others slept in their wagons, remaining wet or, at the least, damp from the rain. We did not feel up to class tonight.

We had some dry wood that we used to start our cookfires under canvas when possible. Everyone was able to eat hot food, although many had to sit in their wagons or under the pine trees due to lack of space under the canvas.

"Tomorrow will be a long day," Brad announced.

Now that we were out of the Umpqua Creek area and the "dreaded Umpqua Canyon" (as it was called in 1846 by Oregon Trail emigrants), we would be moving quickly, moving against the challenge of the weather and less food available for us and our animals. Although, the animals were enjoying the current abundance of grass tonight. After crossing a desert and passing through a rock wall where neither had grass, I could see why they were in a pleasant frame of mind.

The horses were high lined and hobbled, as were the oxen, milk cows, and goats. Traps were set along the nearby creek. But for the rain, it looked a little like heaven right here with the rolling shades of green hills, a creek rushing down the hillside amidst a backdrop of tall, full trees. "It's beginning to feel like we're getting very close to our new home," Chase said.

During the evening, many of the pine cones were picked from the ground and put into a large kettle. Some of the younger children had volunteered to shake them out tonight to harvest the flavorful seeds.

Cordelia and Solomon, as well as Betha and Titus, came over to talk with us. "Do you have any idea where you're going to settle?" they asked. "Are you going all the way north on the trail, or settling somewhere before that?"

Chase and I shared that we liked what we saw right here. We felt that another day or two of travel would provide a better barometer of what we would do.

"Wherever we homestead," we said, "we would like more population. In addition, of course, we want running water, a good grazing area, and trees to provide wood for building our home."

"We also like what we see," Solomon and Cordelia said. "We're planning on being married within the next couple of days before picking our new location."

Their parents had shared with the couples that it would not be proper for them to set up together before they were properly married.

Chase and I and our traveling companions discussed this a little further before we went in a group to talk to Brad. All of us wanted to be married tomorrow after we settled in camp for the day. That would allow us to peel away from the others if we found the right location to homestead without slowing the remaining travelers.

Brad would perform the rites for the separate couples. Our excitement was the same as any engaged couple's would be. We hurried off with wide smiles and details running through our heads to spread the news of our engagements and pending nuptials to the other travelers and family members.

Earlier I had teased Chase and the others that it must have been the baths that we took that gave us all the urge to get married. Chase smiled and said, "I would have married you, dirt and all."

A combination of a hot meal and the excitement of our marriage tomorrow warmed us. We donned large smiles and took quick, confident steps back to our wagons to speak more privately with our betrotheds. It was the perfect time for another kiss as we said our good nights.

I dug through my trunk for something dressier to wear for my big day tomorrow. I found a wide, rose-colored satin ribbon for my hair and a delicate white lace handkerchief that my Mama had given me to carry when I married. She did not specify that it was just for one marriage. I pulled the only other dress that I had from my trunk and pressed it with my hand before hanging it from the inside bow of my wagon, hoping some of the wrinkles would fall out. I picked up my Bible. *I want this in my hands instead of flowers.* My little traveling companion slept through my prowling, as well as the happy sniffles that had seemed to overtake me.

Sleep came easily tonight as I laid my head down and closed my weary eyes.

The next morning brought more misty rain with spots of sunshine just out of our reach.

Jesse Gill came by my wagon and asked if I could assist Almira in her female duties this morning. Her arm was so bruised and swollen from the severe jostling, that she couldn't use it very well. Of course, I went straight away to her wagon. I took some cloth wrappings and wrapped her arm firmly, then applied bag balm to her swollen lip. Then I helped her to her duties. "The wrapping and balm both make me feel better," she said. While riding today, she would rest her arm in her lap on a pillow. I noticed that when she walked, she held it with her other hand.

The weather, although dreary, held the assurance that out ahead we were going to a land of promise. We had traveled the entire day through a tapestry of green and yellow, rolling hills, and, sometimes, sharp outcroppings. We passed loose streams and the promise of creeks near small and large stands of trees, many of which I did not recognize.

Still, we wearied, as did our stock. The distance never ended. There was always another mountain, desert, river, or rock to get through.

Lord give me patience. Don't let me give up now. Today is my wedding day. Please let this be a start to a new life with Chase in our new home, wherever that might be.

We kept moving in the direction of the sun without stopping until early afternoon. Brad announced that we were stopping for the day in recognition of and preparation for the nuptials for three couples.

Our wagons circled in a large open area with a hillside wrapped in forest. We set up our campfires, took care of our animals, and filled our stewpots with venison, onions, sage, and dried squash.

Canvas tarps were once again strung between wagons and under tree branches to give extra protection against the rain. A dressing room of sorts was created for the "brides" to dress and await their entrance. Brad was performing the ceremony with all three of the betrothed couples standing forward with him. He would marry all three couples simultaneously. Each couple stepped forward as he recited their names, making it more personal to each of them.

The brides had no idea that they might need a wedding dress when they left their homes. All in attendance learned a valuable lesson that day. It didn't matter about their clothes and earthly possessions of which they had little or none.

As each young woman joined her betrothed, the crowd murmured quietly and smiled. The young women were lovely, even in their everyday housedresses. Each had taken the time to fix her hair, with the help of the other brides, adding ribbons, dusting their dresses, or pulling another dress out. They carried their family Bible, handkerchief, or other "something borrowed." But most of all, it was the glow and the smile that covered their young and expectant faces as they came forward. They reflected their excitement about starting fresh with their husbands in a territory that was becoming more promising each passing day. As beautiful as their faces were in anticipation, they were enhanced by the sunshine that had pushed the clouds aside and shined down on them. New beginnings were looking pretty good.

When the service ended, everyone was congratulating, shaking hands, hugging, and wishing the young people all the best. Then folks drifted toward their wagons to get their bowls and utensils for their dinners, but not before Brad had asked Evelyn and Martin Linde to move the canned peaches over to a bucket. We were celebrating tonight and would have canned peaches instead of a wedding cake. It seemed only fitting at that time for the new couples to celebrate with a dance. A couple of instruments came out, and the slow dance music began. The first dance being reserved for the newlyweds only.

To be held by Chase and not have to concern myself with what others might say or think was a gift in itself. I could see the other two couples felt the same. When the dance was over, we slowly walked away from the group as Ned and Mary Parker approached us.

"Congratulations," they said. "We appreciate how helpful you've been with our family. We have no problem moving our youngest child out of your wagon at night to allow you more privacy as a married woman."

Chase smiled at me and nodded his head. We had already discussed this. I told the Parkers our suggestion. They could put their youngest and two more of their children in my wagon at night. If only for a couple of nights, and I would be in my husband's wagon. During the day, we would have the same arrangement. We also told them that we didn't know how long this arrangement would last, because we were already interested in the landscape we were seeing. The Parkers were happy for us and accepted our offer for two more of their children to bunk in my wagon. Mary had her hands full with the other children and baby Nikolus.

We left camp early the next day with our sights and our wagon wheels turned to the north as we each continued our search for "Eden."

I've already found mine in Chase.

We traveled for a long time that day and for several following days. We were trying to recover the time spent on our wedding celebrations while being mindful of the weather. At times, we spread our wagons out to cover unencumbered land. This gave each of us a new view and allowed us to cover more ground. As we approached a narrower landscape, we constricted into a serpentine line of wagons until the next opportunity for us to spread out again.

Our course was taking us into a lush area with fast-flowing streams and rivers. If it sounded like easy travel, it was not. Although it was easier and more comfortable than going through rock canyons, crossing deserts, and chopping our way through brush.

The soil was saturated in some areas, especially closer to the rivers or streams. At times it made our wheels bog down in mud, creating more work for our oxen. As much as we wanted to keep the river in sight, we aimed further away from the river. We tried to lessen the load by having folks walk. But we realized very quickly that the mud held them prisoner at times as it caked on their boots, the bottoms of the trousers, and dresses. The little ones rode in the wagons.

For three days, we traveled in rain, sometimes more rigorous than at other times. We found that the weather seemed to change by the minute. We stalwartly traveled through fields and low mountain ranges. The winter runoff the rivers was fast and high, so we chose to take routes where we did not have to cross the river, even with the assistance of rafts.

The news today was great. Dennis was back from his scouting to the north. "I've been to the end of the Applegate Trail," he said, smiling as he explained the territory ahead. "Tomorrow we will come into an area that has some settlers, a welcome sight, indeed. A family by the name of Skinner had claimed 640 acres, built a home in 1845, and moved into their cabin in 1846."

Dennis also relayed to us that he met some of the local Indians. They were hesitant about meeting him and talking to him. Mister Skinner introduced Dennis to a man, a Kalapoya, who appeared to be a mixture of tribes. They were farmers, hunters, and gatherers who lived off the land.

Skinner said they would be affected by the westward movements. Kalapoya, as well as other tribes of Native Americans, were heavily hit by the white man's diseases such as malaria, measles, and smallpox. It added insult to injury that the white man would now be claiming acres of land that had been available to the Kalapoya in the past. And yet, it was reported that the Kalapoya man was calm. Skinner seemed to have established a somewhat congenial relationship with him. I hoped it was that way with the entire tribe. Evidently, they had traded food at times as natives passed by.

They told Dennis that they had originally planned to build the cabin closer to the river. The Kalapoya man was the one who issued a friendly warning to Skinner to move it back. Otherwise, it would flood. The river currently passed over the first site that Skinner chose.

Skinner said that as we traveled north, there were a few other settlers close by. He shared that we travelers would be welcome to stop for a respite tomorrow as we traveled by. He was sure his wife would enjoy the company of someone other than him and their small children. He also wanted to catch up on the events happening in the world.

It stopped raining late afternoon, a perfect time to make camp and construct canvas protection. We had parked our wagon more toward the hillside in an attempt to avoid the heavily saturated ground closer to the river. Gathering dry wood from our wagons, we started our fires to prepare supper. The traps were set, and Chase joined two good riflemen who went into the trees to find some fresh meat. I sent my young traveling companion to his family wagon, noting that he was really missing the attention of his parents and siblings. The animals were thoroughly enjoying the grass during these last days of travel.

Titus, without his own wagon, and Betha, had kept their travel arrangements the same for now, but shared the evening meal and connected each day as often as they could manage. Cordelia made the transition to Solomon's wagon, and they were establishing their daily routine as married folks.

I'm ready to stop for good. I've been on a trail of some sort for six months. Those who came from Missouri have traveled longer. I understand what Evelyn Linde is going through, especially with her being on the trail longer and losing everything. I feel bad for thinking poorly of her for complaining.

Each day I watch the scenery change to a gentler land. One that I could live on. Chase is feeling the same way. We're ready to stop traveling and start living our new lives. Tomorrow when we head toward a settlement of sorts, our eyes and ears will be wide open.

Chapter Thirty

Expectation was on everyone's face today. Not only were we traveling another day closer to our future homes, we were going visiting, as newlyweds! We would be stopping at the Skinner home today and were looking forward to seeing a home without a canvas stretched from the sides or the roof. Something with real wood, permanent and strong, with a fireplace to cook on.

We had a river crossing before getting to Skinners cabin. We crossed in the bend where the water was slowed down and not so deep. It was very cold, so everyone rode on a horse that could, others in the wagons. Once we were out of the water, each oxman and rider wiped down their animal's legs and moved on.

Seeing Skinners cabin with the afternoon sun shining on it was amazing. I understood what would encourage this family to settle right here, even with the hint of unfriendlies.

The cabin was no bigger than 400 square feet, which seemed palatial to my wagon, which had less than 40 square feet. It was made from logs and from what the Mrs. told us, up until recently, had no door or windows.

It was inviting, a place to rest a weary body and to stay dry. The Skinners had real coffee and hot teapots ready within minutes. They invited all of us to come through and see their place, a few at a time, of course. They also invited us to camp on their land that night.

Chase took my hand and led me out to our wagon, looking at me while I glanced all around, not wanting to miss anything. The Skinners had managed to mark their 640 acres to each side of them. They had most recently built a small shed next to a corral, so as to protect their livestock, feed, and farming implements.

I was not sure how we communicated this, but we eventually got the attention of Brad and Dennis. We got on saddle horses and rode out a couple of miles before turning back. According to Dennis, there was another cabin down the way and back a bit. There were more homes on the other side of the river, within 10 miles.

We felt like we were within reach of our dreams, that we had traversed this rough, sometimes unyielding, land to get where the good Lord intended us to be. Brad took that time to hand us a written note showing that he had performed our nuptials while on the trail. It had the date and his signature stating that it was legal and binding. This would be very important when it came time for us to claim acreage.

It was hard to sleep that night with the excitement of the tiny, sparse settlement filling up our thoughts. Cordelia and Solomon came by Chase's wagon after class was finished. They had been quietly holding hands and whispering as they approached. Cordelia, being very open and communicative, jumped right into the conversation. They really liked this area and knew that we had gone out to observe. They asked our thoughts on the location and the land, and wanted to know if we were giving serious consideration to living here. We told them that we thought very well of everything, especially since there were already a few homes built and the Indians hadn't hurt them. Tomorrow we would make a decision as we traveled past the land where we wanted to stay.

It felt like our wedding day once again with the sun shining down against the backdrop of the distant hills and burnished trees. The wagons spread out as we rolled, trying to avoid making heavy ruts of mud. The soil here seemed to have very good drainage. There were occasional stands of trees, enough for building materials for a modest home.

We came over a small incline with my wagon and Chase's almost side by side, positioning us to catch the view together as we peaked the small hill.

Eyes big, smiles bigger, we stopped at the very same time and stared ahead. It was like a painted picture. Everything was there that we needed to start our new lives together. We nodded to each other in a show of agreement.

Cordelia and Solomon sat behind us, smiling. We pulled our three wagons and two saddle horses out of the lineup and waved to Brad and our other companions. Brad rode back to join us, and others pulled their wagons up and stopped. They flowed over the wagon seats and out of the back of wagons and aimed for us with hugs and good wishes. We shook hands and heartily patted our friends on the back. Some more than others. Betha and Titus made a point of telling us that when they could get a wagon or some conveyance of their own, they just might be returning to set up their own household close by.

We offered, to most, to come for a visit. Or, at the very least, to send word where they settled.

As they headed north, we rolled toward the slight hill to park and set up our home.

About the Author

OREGON FIRST CLAIMED LINDA'S heart in 1980 when she and her family moved there. It was no surprise, based on her past involvements in her community, that in 1993 she became very immersed in planning for the Oregon and Applegate Trail celebrations. It was the 150th Anniversary, touted as the Sesquicentennial of each, Oregon in 1993 and Applegate in 1996. Tourism departments throughout the involved states banded together to support events, including a wagon train that started in Winnemucca, Nevada.

Linda, being the Visitors and Convention Bureau Director at the time, as well as a member on the Oregon Trail Board of Directors and the Applegate Trail Coalition, was involved in the planning process and support. She traveled on a wagon 31 days during the 51-day trip, as she served as Quartermaster for the west side.

There are a number of highway and park markers, as well as museums, that have been built to encourage our communities to learn more of our area history.

In 1996, Linda received the Frank Branch Riley Heritage Tourism Award from Travel Oregon, Oregon's Travel & Tourism Industry Award. She decided at that time that she needed to write her own story, as real and as rich as many of the "characters" that she became acquainted with, either by their diaries or the reenactment.

Linda moved to Tombstone, Arizona, for about three years, where her love of the West was accelerated. She wandered ghost towns, metal detected on the desert, dressed as a local character of the 1800's, (many who live there dress in period costume when in town), and immersed in the history of the Southwest.

A huge part of the "old west" history that caught her interest is that of the Native Americans. She was able to research her Cherokee history and how it related to other tribes that are prevalent in both the South, as well as the Northwest. She still dances in POW WOW's and proudly wears her heritage.

Linda lives in Southern Oregon, where she spends her time enjoying dancing, reading, gardening, attending POW WOW's and, of course, writing.

This is Linda's first novel.

Contact the Author

You can email Linda Lochard at lstoryteller0@gmail.com. Please visit and follow her on Facebook.com/LindaLochard-Author.